My Brother's Keeper

TJ Lee

DEDICATION

To those awesome siblings who just can't give up on their loved ones, even when the world already has. You are a role model to us all.

Prologue

Fiona

"Tonight is going to be ep-ic." I rolled my eyes at Katia as she moved both hands through the air, as though she were outlining a lit-up sign. Most likely imagining her name in lights.

"Oh yeah, and why is that?" I was only pretending to be ignorant. I knew exactly what she was talking about.

She'd spoken of nothing else for weeks. And the look she gave me was worth it. My smile cracked at her "I will kill you if you are serious" look.

"Fi…."

My smile turned into full-blown giggles as we walked down the hall. "I'm just messing with you."

Katia was the one rolling her eyes this time. "I can't believe you. Tonight is important, Fi. You have to be there for me."

I wiped an amused tear out of my eye as I wrapped an apologetic arm around her shoulder. "I got you, Kat. You know that."

She sighed and we stopped walking. "I know you do. I'm just nervous."

I placed both my hands on her shoulders, forcing her to look at me. "Hey, it's all good. Nothing is going to happen that will mess any of it up. I babysat the twins last night and got 50 for it. Just enough to buy my ticket to the game, and dinner after to celebrate. I will be standing right there on the sidelines, recording every minute of it."

I used to only get half that for babysitting the Walker twins, but ever since the youngest was diagnosed with diabetes, their parents have paid double. The six-year-old terror was not a fan of watching what he ate, whether his brother had to as well or not. They also trained me on how to check blood sugar and give insulin. I figured it was a good life skill to have, you never knew what the future held.

She grunted uncomfortably. "You don't need to record it. Both my parents will be doing that."

I pushed her playfully as we turned to keep walking to our first class. "Girl," I tsked. "I need to have my own copy. Besides, we both know your Dad's hands always shake while holding his phone up for longer than 5 seconds and your mom will be crying, which means she won't be all that steady either."

Plus, I was gonna take my copy, clean it up, and do some fancy stuff with it before I gave it to her for her birthday next week. It didn't matter that it would be recorded with my phone. I had a gift with computers and stuff. For now, computers were just a hobby of mine, but one day…

Katia agreed with a shy grin before we stepped into our first torture session of the day.

A few hours later, I headed toward the lunch area to buy my ticket for tonight's football game - the one my best friend would be singing the National Anthem for - her first time with such a large crowd. I was proud of her. She worked hard for this. I was hoping to make the video epic enough for her to use later, when she finally caved to her real desires to apply for Julliard. Her dream school.

I barely stepped out the double doors that led to the outdoor patio area - a large circular set up with picnic tables, trees, and lots of dead grass, surrounded by the school buildings that housed the classrooms - when I heard the ominous sounds of a fight off to the side. It was more shaded in that area, due to a few larger trees. A perfect place to pick on someone out of the semi-carefully watching school security.

With an eye roll and a head shake, I lifted my foot to keep walking. I was used to the fights the idiots in this school did on the regular. Not my problem.

I stalled though when the words being yelled reached my ears.

"Give me my money, Randy. Or you're dead." A boy's voice growled out.

We had a big school - nearly 3,000 kids -and Randy wasn't all that unique of a name. But something in my gut twisted anyway.

No, not possible. He wouldn't be in a fight. His coach would kill him. I took another step away, then stopped with a sigh. I cursed to myself, spun, and jogged over to the fight.

I pushed my way through the growing crowd just in time to see a large kid, with a pitch-black mohawk, knee another boy in the stomach hard enough to make him fold over. The kid, who was now on the ground, coughed and groaned. I recognized the short brown hair that stuck up in every direction like he forgot to brush it this morning.

Which he probably had. I left earlier than usual this morning since Katia and her mom picked me up. He had been lagging, so he drove in on his own. Which also meant I wasn't there to remind the nitwit to do little things… like brushing his hair.

"I ain't got it." Randy coughed some more, trying to push himself off the ground to stand back up. As shaky as his legs were, I was pretty sure he had been hit more than once already. "Not yet."

The much larger kid pushed him back over with his foot and leaned over him with a sneer. "You made the bet. You promised to pay it back last week. You didn't." He pulled his leg back and swung it forward, right into Randy's rib cage. Making him gasp for air.

"Stop!!" I yelled, unable to stand by and let any more harm come to him. I ran forward to stand between the two boys, raising my hands to stop the bully from causing further damage. "Stop. Please."

He sneered at me before glancing down at Randy again. "You'd be wise to dump his lazy A and get yourself a new boyfriend. He's worthless."

I lowered my arms with a defeated sigh. "He's not my boyfriend. He's my brother."

"Go away, Fi. I can handle this." Randy moaned as he tried to push himself up off the ground once again.

I glared at him. "Yeah, you're doing a bang-up job of handling things all right." I turned back to the boy who now had his arms crossed over his chest, a smug look on his face. And a creepy interest in his eyes. I held back the grimace when I noticed the metal spikes along his eyebrows.

"Sister, huh?" He stepped closer to me, blatantly checking me out now. "Guess you got all the looks as well as the brains. I bet you and me can work out a deal." He lifted his hand and picked up a small piece of my long brown hair that was over my shoulder.

I shuttered and stepped away from him. "You're disgusting. How much does he owe you?"

Not caring about the rebuff, the boy grinned. "40 bucks. Course, I'd be willing to take it in trade."

"I'm sure you would." I pulled my wallet out of my bag and opened it. Closing my eyes in defeat, I pulled out the two twenties. It left me with only ten dollars. Thankfully, the game ticket would only cost me seven. I wouldn't be able to go out and celebrate with Katia, but I could still be there for her big moment. I shoved the money into the brute's hand, glaring at him with all my might.

"Paying for it is probably the only way you get any with that angry scowl on your face all the time. Take the money and leave him be. Your debt is settled."

He counted the cash and winked at me. "Pleasure doing business with you. If you change your mind…"

"I won't." I cut him off as I turned to help Randy straighten up.

He had mostly made it back onto his feet and was now leaning against the tree, his lip bleeding and the black eye forming. With a sad sigh, I put an arm around his waist and helped him stand straighter.

The crowd had already dispersed since there was nothing of interest to watch anymore. I helped my big brother stumble over to the closest picnic table.

"What happened, Randy?"

"I bet on the school's football team. I honestly didn't think they would make it to the finals." He chuckled, then groaned from the pain.

"Dad is going to be so ticked when he sees you."

Randy snorted. "Please, he won't even notice."

Sadly, that was probably true. Ever since our mother died last year, our father had basically shut down.

"Why did you have to make a stupid bet?"

He shrugged. His nonchalant attitude worried me. What was he hiding?

There was only so much I could do when it came to trying to save my family. What little I had left of it. Before mom died, she made me promise to keep the family together. To not let the men of the family fall apart completely. Desperate to see her smile one last time, I agreed. Even though I often wished I hadn't.

When Mom died, she took my childhood with her.

Every night, I made sure Dad drank at least some water and ate actual food. Every morning, I made sure he had coffee to help him get up and go to work on time (and somewhat sober). I cleaned the house and cooked dinner every day. I did the shopping, with whatever money my father remembered to put in the shopping jar when he got paid.

Randy seemed to be holding up fine. At least I thought he had. He was still wrestling, and he was passing all of his classes. When he was home, he was typically in his room. I usually only saw him in passing, both at school and at home. And when we carpooled in the car we shared.

"Do you want me to help you get to the nurse? That eye looks like it could use an ice pack." I offered, knowing questioning him further about the bet would do no good. At one time Randy and I had been close, but as time moved on, he pushed me away.

He started to laugh sardonically, then moaned, and placed a hand on his ribs. They were probably bruised. Mohawk had been wearing some pretty heavy boots.

"No, they'll just make me report it to the office. I'll be fine."

With an eye roll, I stepped away. "I will get it and tell them it is for me. I'll say I have cramps or something. Stay here. I'll be right back."

I didn't give him a chance to argue, I just turned and walked away. A minute later, I was about to pass the ticket table and stopped. Torn, I glanced back at Randy, who had already been joined by a couple of other boys. He'd survive. He owed me anyway.

I quickly bought my ticket to the game, then continued on to the health office.

Thankfully, they were busy. Which meant they did not question me when I told them I slammed my fingers in the bathroom stall door and needed an ice pack - odds were I would actually need one for cramps next week. They just reached into a drawer and grabbed one. They twisted it a few times and then handed the disposable ice pack to me before turning to the next kid.

Randy was laughing with his friends when I returned, like nothing had happened. I walked up and shoved the ice pack on his eye, a little roughly, making the other boys laugh.

Randy caught my hand as I moved to leave them. He smiled softly and squeezed my wrist with affection. "Thanks, Fi. You're the best sister."

He was a butthead. I melted and smiled back, giving him a small nod. It was nice to see a small glimpse of the boy I used to know.

The bell rang not much later, before I even had a chance to grab something to eat. I jogged over to one of the kids who I knew sold snacks out of his backpack and handed him one of the few bills I had left in exchange for a bag of chips. All he had left was plain Cheetos. Which I was fine with since I didn't care for the hot ones anyway.

After school, Katia waited near my class anxiously. We had separate lunches, so I hadn't seen her since our first-period class ended. I lifted my game ticket up and she squealed. I laughed with her as we boarded the bus home. I didn't mention anything about Randy or the debt I paid for him. I didn't want to do anything that would ruin her day.

That night, I stood on the sidelines with her parents. All three of us recorded with our phones, while Katia belted out the National Anthem at the first round of finals. The crowd cheered - because my best friend had the best voice in the world. It had nothing to do with me being biased either - which I totally was - she had tried out and earned her placement there.

We left before the game even started. Her parents surprised us both by taking us out to eat. Their treat. I sighed with relief. Katia never needed to know my brother almost ruined her night. She wasn't his biggest fan to begin with. Never had been. I didn't really know why, nor did I care. It didn't affect my relationship with either of them.

Randy ended up getting his arm broken a few weeks later.

By the same guy.

Sadly, they both knew who would pay the debt.

I was grateful when my brother left for college at the end of the school year. I still had two more years to go, but I had my plans. As soon as I turned 16, I got a work permit from school and started working at a local movie theater. I was planning to save everything I could up for college. I worked as often as they would let me.

I thought I would get a reprieve once Randy was gone. I thought I would no longer have to be his keeper, paying off his debts.

I thought wrong.

I had already started a bad habit of helping him out.

No one but me knew about his gambling problem, and I wanted to keep it that way. I just had to keep faith that eventually he would kick the habit.

Chapter 1

Fiona

I paused outside the hospital room door, ignoring the nurses walking behind me, and the sounds of family members leaving the rooms up and down the hall. The place had that feeling of winding down for the day. It wasn't all that noticeable. Not unless you had spent enough time there to know the difference.

Sadly, I had. I'd spent the majority of the past week in this very room. Only leaving to go home and shower once in a while.

Today had been my first day back at work. Physically anyway. The joy of cyber security - it was easy to work remotely. Considering I'd been at my job for 7 years, my bosses trusted me enough to know I would actually be working when I asked to work out of the office.

I jump-startled when a soft hand landed on my arm. Nurse Betty, with her red hair mostly still in its bun, stood next to me.

"You all right, darling?"

I gave her a soft smile, something I didn't fully feel. It had felt good being back in my own life. Even if it was for only a few hours. Unfortunately, that made it ten times harder to go back into that depressing room.

"Yeah, Betty. Just taking a moment before I go in. I want to make sure I don't bring any outside stress in there with me."

She patted my arm a couple of times before removing it. "I understand. It's hard going back and forth. But the doctor says he'll be able to go home in a day or two."

I closed my eyes and sighed. "That's good news." Not.

I mean, yes obviously it was. I loved him and I wanted him home. It just meant more work for me in the long run.

With one more sigh, and a supportive pat on the shoulder from Nurse Betty, I pushed my way through the door.

I couldn't help but smile at the grin he gave me from where he lay on the bed. Up until about three years ago, I rarely saw the man smile. Since then, though, they started coming more often. This last week, they'd been brighter than I remembered seeing since I was a little kid.

As happy as I was to see it, I wished he hadn't had to go through all of this to get that part of him back.

"Hey, Pixie. How was work?"

I chuckled. That was another thing that had returned. The nickname. A little girl goes through one very short phase of loving fairies and dressing up like them every chance she could, and a new nickname is born.

Leave it to Dads to be embarrassing.

"Great. I was so worried I had fallen behind, but it was like I hadn't ever left." Except for all the hugs and well-wishers.

Everybody had offered their support and told me they missed having me around. Probably because I usually did most of the work, always helping them out once I was done with my own. And sometimes at the same time as my own.

His grin crinkled his aging face. "I'm glad to hear it. I'm so proud of you for sticking with it and not giving up."

Dad was referring to college. He was still under the belief that I worked so many hours to help pay for my schooling, instead of taking out a bunch of student loans. Little did he know, I still took out most of it in loans. I had only worked so much to try and keep my brother above water. I also borrowed more than needed because of him.

Randy ended up losing his scholarship half way through college because he missed a lot of practices and was failing most of his classes. And, on occasion, he'd show up to one or both with bruises he always lied about. Now he was a manager for the movie theater, the same one I had worked at all through high school and college.

That had not been fun.

The most embarrassing moment of my life happened while working with my brother.

With no social life, I only met new people through work. Not a problem usually. It was during my summer between high school and college when Randy started there. I was dating a coworker, one of the temporary employees to get us through the busy summer season.

On occasion, we would sneak into one of the theaters not being used, usually because they were between showings, and were scheduled for cleaning. We were both on break, and found a dark, empty room, and a good corner.

You see where I am going with this?

Both our shirts were on the floor, and we were in the process of losing our pants. Both were open wide, but you couldn't see any part of me, since Bobby's hand was fully covering me, inside and out. His knees were bending, as his kisses were moving further south, when the lights flashed on suddenly. We still had twenty minutes before that room was due to be cleaned.

I didn't register what the lights coming on meant, seeing as I was right on the edge of the highlight of my evening, when my brother's deep voice rang through the fog, yelling "my eyes, my eyes!" Repeatedly. At least he had the decency to run back out and close the door before his partner came in after him.

Needless to say, I did not go over that edge. Not until work was over and we were in Bobby's car. Fully alone. And even then, he had to work to get me to relax. We also never hid in an empty theater again.

"Thanks, Daddy." I pushed unwanted memories away and focused on him. His voice was still weak, but better. "How are you feeling? How was your day?"

I leaned down and kissed my Dad's pale cheeks. At least they had a little more color today. I sat down in the chair next to his bed, the one I'd practically been living in for the last week.

Dad took my hand in his and patted it softly. That was a good sign. Two days ago, he wouldn't have been able to pat me.

"It was a good day. I had a nice long talk with the doctor and some other people that came in."

"Oh, yeah. What other people?"

He looked to be taking a deep breath, like he was preparing for something. It kind of freaked me out, but I was pretty good at hiding my emotions around my family by now.

"A representative for Olympus Prime came by to see me today."

I'd heard that name before, but I couldn't remember specifically what it was. He must have seen my confusion since I didn't care to try and hide that one. He reached for the dining tray attached to the bed and picked up a brochure. On the cover was an older man playing chess with a younger man who was wearing scrubs.

"A retirement home? I thought you never wanted to live in one of those places."

He had never been quiet about his opinion of them. In fact, I was pretty sure that was one reason why he quit drinking a few years ago. He claimed it was because he was trying to stay healthy.

"Not exactly. While it is for retirees, it's also a nursing home." His face looked so sad when he said that.

"Dad, what did the doctor say today?" He had to have said something, considering this had never come up before.

"He said a whole bunch of medical stuff that I don't even remember. But what it comes down to is the fact that I am never going to be the same again. All my years of drinking really did a number on my body. If I hadn't quit when I had, I probably wouldn't have survived the heart attack. If I'm not extremely careful, I could have a worse one, or even a stroke."

I squeezed his hands, trying to support him and remind myself he was still there. "That's what you have me for. Katia and I already made a plan. She is going to help me find someone to sublease my apartment. I am going to move home and take care of you. If you need more care, we can hire a home health-aide. At least for during the day, when I have to go into the office."

He tsked and shook his head. "No, Pixie. You've given up enough of your life to take care of me. I have it all worked out. Between you, me, and Katia, we can get all this settled by the time I am released."

While there was a lot I wanted to argue with, it was the last bit that stopped me short. "Katia?"

"Yes, while I have enough in my retirement from the plant, as well as my social security and what's left of your mom's life insurance, I want to make sure that you never get stuck paying for my bills. So…" He gulped silently. I recognized the look. It was the one he got anytime he was thinking about mom. "So, I want to sell the house. I figured Katia would be someone we could trust to help us get the best deal that we can."

She definitely would. When Katia was pregnant with her first baby - her husband had refused to let her work while pregnant - she decided to take a couple real estate classes. It wasn't long after that she got her license. Now she was ranked as one of the best Real Estate Agents in Los Angeles. Which was why she was going to help me find someone to sublease.

I wouldn't say it to my father, but him being in a nursing home would be a big relief for me. "Are you sure that is what you want? Selling our home, and moving into a nursing home?"

He shrugged. "It's just me there now. It can be kind of lonely at night. Besides, it kind of feels like going back to college again, only without all the boring classes."

I laughed with him. "Okay. If this is what you want. But know, if you change your mind, I can move back home with you."

"No." He said sharply, then quickly softened his tone with a smile. "You've done too much for me. For us. You think I don't know how much of the family weight you have carried since your mother died? I've always known how much you've done for us. And some nights, it made me feel worse than I already did. My teenage daughter having to take care of me?" He shook his head, disappointed in himself. "No, Pixie. The least I can do for you is to take some of that weight off. And, honestly, the place doesn't sound so bad. Which leads me to one thing I do need your help with, only for legal purposes of course. At least for now."

"What's that?"

"Tomorrow, my lawyer is going to come by." It took a little more work to control my auto-response to that bomb. "I want to give you Power of Attorney… just in case. This will also give you access to my bank accounts and such. You can help me set up those automatic payment things for the few bills I will still have."

"But… Randy…"

"May be the oldest," he cut me off, already knowing where I was going with that, "but he isn't exactly the best with money. I may not know all the details, nor do I want to, but that boy just can't seem to keep a hold of money. I know you help him out from time to time because you are a good sister, but Pixie, it's about time to let that boy deal with his own problems."

I bit my lip and looked at my lap. I knew that. I always knew that. But I also had a soft spot for the idiot.

"I know, Daddy. And one day, I will. I just haven't reached that point yet."

He huffed. "Yeah, I know that too. The least I can do is force you to reach that point with me. I want you to have a life outside of work and the family. I want you to push further with work. Reach for the stars." He winked at me and smiled. "Just don't forget about your old man and come visit me once in a while."

I giggled softly and moved to lay my head on his shoulder. "I could never forget about you, Daddy."

Time flew quickly. I blinked, and Dad was getting situated in his new little apartment. The first time I visited, just two days later, I found him laughing with an old friend from the plant. They were living only one floor apart. My Dad was already more alive than I had seen in over a decade.

I blinked again, and Katia and I were cleaning out the house, and the new buyers were in escrow. Randy said he'd come help us, but I wasn't holding my breath.

I had been there for a little over an hour when Katia arrived. I opened the door to my best friend, my ride or die, and then laughed. She held up two bottles of champagne and was wearing jeans and a t-shirt. It was the t-shirt that made me laugh. She had obviously made it herself. It was bright purple and pink tie-died (because Katia was a unique person who randomly liked to tie-dye clothes).

Across the top read *Congrats to my bestie for making partner! That's right cyber spies, look out, because she's got her cyber eye on you.* The lettering got smaller and smaller as it went through.

Her husband bought her a Cricket last year. He and I both agreed it had not been the brightest of ideas. She loved it a little too much. And now they had their names and random phrases on literally every material in their house.

"Congrats, Fi!!!" Katia lifted her champagne filled hands in the air and moved in for a hug.

"Congrats on what?"

Katia stepped back from me, as we both turned toward the deep voice. Shockingly, Randy had arrived. And on time.

I cleared my throat nervously. I always felt a little bad that my dreams were coming true and his weren't. "I, uh, got a promotion at work. It's no big deal."

Katia snorted and rolled her eyes at me. "They made her a Junior partner. That's a big freaking deal, Fi."

I blushed. It was a big deal, but I wasn't used to being treated like that. I was completely blindsided when they approached me the week before, saying I was in the running. I had been a nervous wreck when I sat down with the Senior partners for a "talk." I thought for sure they were going to pass me up, especially with how much time off I had taken recently. But no. They had seen it all differently. Not only was I family oriented, but I proved that I could still balance my work load, while taking care of my family.

Go figure.

It also brought to light how much of everyone else's work I usually ended up helping with - cough, cough, Chris, cough, cough.

"Wow, Fi. That's awesome. Congrats." Randy wrapped me in a warm hug. "I'm so proud of you, sis." He sounded like he actually meant it too.

"Thanks." I croaked, making them both laugh.

We spent the next few hours packing up everything in the house, creating piles for storage, give-away, and what we would take with us. Even Katia was going to take a few things, mostly for her girls – and to pass onto me when I was ready. *If* I was ever ready for my own.

By the time we decided food was a necessity, we were all covered in dust and sweat. We sat around the dining room table, probably for the last time before it got put into storage for who knows how long, and munched on a couple pizzas, wings, and breadsticks. Katia, like the mother she was, would not let us have the brownie-cookies until we finished our dinner.

"So, what all is going to be different with the promotion?" Randy asked, taking a big bite of his Meat Lovers.

I shrugged, finishing my bite of the Hawaiian. "Not much really. I get a bigger office, which is kind of cool, since I'm moving up a floor. I will have a handful of people reporting to me, and I will report directly to a Senior partner. That part I could live without."

Katia giggled. "Hopefully after being around them so much, they will stop freaking you out all the time."

I rolled my eyes. "One could only hope."

We each updated the others on our changes in life. I was thrilled to realize that Randy seemed to actually enjoy his job. He was even considering trying to move up to a district level position. I was proud that he was making a real go of it there.

It was long past dark when Katia left us, she purposely waited until after bedtime to return to her husband and two daughters. She didn't even lie about it, she flat out said that was why she stayed so long.

Randy and I stood in the living room filled with boxes, all waiting for the movers to come the next day, just staring at the place we grew up in.

"It's weird knowing we will never be back here after tomorrow. Knowing someone else will be raising their family here." Knowing someone else's mother would be living here. I couldn't say that one out loud, it was hard enough just thinking about it.

"Yeah, it is. I'm gonna miss this place. I almost wish we weren't selling. I mean I totally get why, and I agree it was a good call, but still… ya know?"

I sighed and wrapped my arms around his left arm, hugging my big brother. The nostalgia for the good ole days was getting to me.

"Yeah, I do. As badly as I wanted to argue with Dad, it was kind of a relief at the same time."

Randy snorted. "I bet."

All was silent, the feeling of unspoken subjects lying between us. Randy knew about the whole deal with Dad and the Power of Attorney thing. He had popped in for a random hospital visit while the lawyer was still there. The lawyer and I both felt awkward and nervous while Dad explained the new set up to him. Randy and I hadn't spoken about it since. We hadn't really spoken about Dad much either. Family dinners in the nursing home lately had been kind of subdued. When my big brother bothered to come anyway.

"I understand why he did it. I agree with that one too."

I turned to look at him, surprised. So many surprises tonight. "You do?"

"Yeah. I really do. I don't have the best history with money." His voice trailed off, and a new edge took over his face. One I recognized a little too well.

"You were doing so good, Randy."

"I know. But after Dad's heart attack, and then all the changes. I thought maybe I could help. I've been getting by with playing online, with fake money. It helped with the itch. I do really good, so I thought I'd try again. I found a new place, very low key, not many people."

Sadly, I laid my head on his shoulder, not knowing what else to do. And knowing I couldn't look at him. "How bad is it?"

I felt his shoulder move under me as he shrugged. "Just 5. I stopped when I realized how low I was getting."

I closed my eyes to hide the eye roll. Right, because he didn't think 5,000 in the hole was all that deep. And of course, it was the exact amount I got as a bonus for my promotion. Figures.

Did he hear Katia ask me about the bonus earlier? He had been in his old room while we were in mine. At least I thought he was in there.

"I may not know all the details, nor do I want to, but that boy just can't seem to keep a hold of money. I know you help out from time to time because you are a good sister, but Pixie, it's about time to let that boy deal with his own problems." My Dad's deep and shaky voice rolled through me.

Randy did need to face his own consequences, I knew that. And I was sure he knew that. But we also both knew I wasn't to the point of giving up on him. At least he wouldn't wipe out my savings this time. Close, but not quite.

"I can give it to you."

He blew out a relieved breath, making me wonder what these people would have done if he hadn't been able to pay them back.

"Thanks, Fi."

Instead of verbally responding, I kissed his sweaty shirt sleeve then moved away to do one more walk down memory lane.

Chapter 2

Dillan

I raised an eyebrow as one of my dancers sauntered up next to where I leaned against the back wall. I liked to rotate where I kept an eye on my business. Especially on nights like tonight. These were big money nights, well one of them. My club was popular every night, no matter the day. But it was my *other* endeavors that brought in the real money.

I opened an arm, allowing Bunny to slide up next to me, putting on a show for the customers. She was one of the few dancers who did more than dance. We both wanted the customers to see how close they could get to her.

Bunny took it a step further, leaning in like she was going to kiss my jaw, but was really moving in to whisper in my ear.

"Undercover chick in the club."

I smiled softly, lifting a hand to move her blonde hair behind her ear. All of my people knew how to spot cops, no matter how they dressed.

"And do we know who her target is?"

Bunny trailed a finger down my chest, playing with the buttons on my black dress shirt. "Looks like it might be Bruno. He is here with a client."

I sighed and straightened my position, keeping my arm around her waist. She looked up at me, a hunger in her eyes. Unfortunately, I kept a firm line between business and pleasure, much to her dismay.

"Where?"

The dark red painted lips pouted. "Far end of the bar. Black hair, braided. Tiny black dress with bomb red heels."

I leaned down and kissed her cheek, at the same time I squeezed her moneymaker which was barely wrapped in a red leather skirt. Bunny squeaked, then broke out giggling as I moved away from her. I knew it wouldn't be long before someone took my position with her. She was my most popular private dancer for a reason.

I took a long walk around the outskirts of the club, circling all the customers dancing in the middle of the room around my dancer in faux cages on top of small islands.

I passed by the stage where my in-house DJ was doing his own version of dancing. I nodded to my stage security. There would be no point in talking to them, seeing as they had expensive earplugs to help protect their ears from the loud speakers surrounding the stage.

Carefully, I made my way to the bar, staying clear of the suspected cop. I stationed myself where I would have a good view of her, but not her of me. It wasn't long before Kent stepped over to me.

"S'up, bossman. You wanna drink?"

"My usual, please."

With a nod, he reached under the bar for the unlabeled bottle, then poured two fingers into a shot glass. He winked as he set it on the bar and moved on to a paying customer.

Warm Coke wasn't my favorite, but it helped sell the image. A dark-colored drink in a mostly dark room was all I needed. While I wouldn't have minded if it was the real thing, especially the way the night was starting, I couldn't afford to lose my head.

I watched as Kent made his way back down the bar, working his way back to the woman of the hour. I chuckled as he made her another Margarita – a virgin. Looks like I wasn't the only one wanting a clear head tonight.

She turned down a half-drunk man while she waited. She smiled and he walked away with a grin. Whatever she said, he backed off without any issue. Not long after she took a sip from her new drink, another man walked up to the bar. He was wearing dark jeans with a black t-shirt. But the lean muscles were a bit telling. As was the way his lips moved, whispering to nobody in particular, from right behind the woman. She whispered something in return, from behind her glass.

Her partner.

When their conversation finished, the woman pushed off her stool and walked away. The man turned and leaned against the bar, a bottle of beer in his hands. He took a long swig of his bottle as she walked away from him. I couldn't help but laugh at the remorseful look on his face as she closed the distance between her and Bruno.

Bruno was at a table with two other men, all three wore expensive suits and were drinking a bottle of our most expensive whiskey. They could afford it.

I cast a quick glance across the room to where I usually saw the Russians. Sure enough, Ivan and his girlfriend of the hour were enjoying the semi-private table. Bruno and his men didn't pay them any attention. I knew they wouldn't. My club was the only one in neutral territory.

I continuously refused to join either of their "families." I preferred my independence. They allowed it, and my extracurricular activities, as long as I did not encroach on their businesses. In return, I allowed them to occasionally broker deals in the dark spaces of my club. I watched their backs, and they generally watched mine. A mutually beneficial arrangement.

Which also meant that I needed to figure out what was going on with these cops and stop it before anything happened. The last thing I needed was for them to ruin this for me.

I waited to see what would happen, wanting to see what the cops' play would be before I made a move. What was their purpose here tonight?

The female cop approached Bruno's side, sliding a hand down the back of his shoulder. He made a show of checking her out before inviting her to sit on his lap, with a large grin. I glanced over to her partner still at the bar, who seemed to be holding his bottle a little too tightly.

Guess I knew her purpose in being here now.

I lifted a finger and Kent came running, cutting off the group of women he was helping. They frowned until they saw me. I needed to get a move on it before they got up the guts to come over here. Normally I wouldn't mind the benefits of owning a nightclub, just not tonight.

"Yes, sir."

"I need a bottle of our best Scotch. Four glasses."

Kent licked his lips nervously, looking around. "Sure. Everything alright?"

"I'm sure it is. I just need to intervene before it turns into something."

He nodded at me, only slightly mollified. It wasn't often the cops came into the club. Come to think of it, it might be Kent's first time. He joined us only a few months ago. I glanced back to Bruno's table, just in time to see his hand slide down to rest on the cop's butt. I had time.

I leaned over the counter to speak softly to my new man. "The man at the end, drinking his beer like he wants to punch a fool. See him?"

Kent nodded.

"Now, see the woman who ordered the virgin margarita sitting on Bruno's lap?"

He lifted to his toes and maneuvered to look around the crowded bar. "Yeah."

"Undercover cops. My guess, it's her job to try and get close to Bruno. Her partner doesn't seem very happy about it."

Kent turned back to me with wide eyes. "How do you know all that?"

I roughly patted his shoulder before picking up the small tray he prepared for me. "You learn to spot them. I'll have someone teach you soon."

His smile was shaky as he moved back to the group of girls. He was a good bartender and handled the mafia presence well. I hoped this didn't screw that up.

Pushing those thoughts aside, I approached Bruno's table with a grin, supporting the tray with my left hand.

"Gentlemen, it's been a while since I've had the pleasure of having a drink with you. Join me?" I laid the tray down in the middle of the table. All three men studied my face, watching me carefully.

"Grazie, Dillan. We'd be honored. How is business?" Bruno wrapped his large hands around the glass I filled in front of him.

"Good, as always. As you can see, we get many different types of people visiting. Nothing like shadows and alcohol to give people the confidence to act out of their nature. Let their hair down, so to speak."

Bruno threw back his shot, then smacked his lips. "Hmmm, that is smooth. You brought us the good stuff." He reached over and filled another glass for himself, then refilled his friends' drinks. His other hand slid up to the female cop's upper back, just enough to support her but not let her know things had changed. "Grazie, my friend. It's nice to know we have a place where we can let our own hair down and know we are safe doing so."

I nodded my head, demonstrating my acceptance and understanding. "Well, gentlemen, I hope you enjoy your night. As always, enjoy your time here at *Indecent*."

I dropped the tray off back at the bar, getting a confused look from Kent. I winked at him and headed toward the back door. Just before leaving, I turned and saw the female cop walking away from Bruno with a very confused look on her face. Her partner, on the other hand, looked relieved. He was doing a poor job of hiding it. They really should find someone else to partner with her on undercover assignments.

With a shake of the head, I stepped out of the dark club room and into a semi-dark, private stairwell. I descended down to the basement level and entered the door on the right. One of the reasons I chose to buy this building for the club was because of the extensive basement. I split it in two, one of the rooms much smaller than the other. Both were soundproofed. Both were equally fruitful.

The smaller room was well lit, but in an aesthetically pleasing way. The room held five poker tables, each filled with three to five people. To the right was a small bar where drinks could be fixed, and money exchanged for chips. I made my way over to the two men standing behind the bar.

"Are we ready?" I asked my long-time friend and right-hand man, Keith.

He picked up his tablet and scrolled. "Just about. We have five for the tournament, and ten that are just here to play like normal."

"That's not bad. So why do you look concerned?"

He cleared his throat and looked toward the center table, the one that had four men and one woman sitting there. It was the man on the end with the unruly brown hair that caught my attention. He was still in decent shape, but it was obvious he hadn't been trying all that recently. I'd known this man for a few years. He was a regular.

He must have felt our eyes on him because he looked up. I just stared, knowing he'd get the hint. Which he did. He apprehensively stood up and walked over. I leaned against the bar, resting my right arm on the top and folded my hands together.

"Hi-yah, Dillan. How are you?"

"Doing good. But I'll be even better once you pay me back."

Randy lifted a hand and scratched the back of his head awkwardly. "I'm working on it, I swear."

"Ya huh. You've given me that line before." I turned my head to look at Keith, keeping my relaxed pose against the bar. "How much are we up to this time?"

He made a show of studying the tablet in his hands, which I knew wasn't needed. Keith was always prepared and knew what I would need. "25, sir."

I whistled and turned back to Randy. "You owe me 25,000, and yet you have the money to enter the special tournament."

Randy shot a look over his shoulder, toward the table he had just come from, before lowering his voice and leaning closer. "Look, we both know I can beat these guys in my sleep. I can win back all of your money tonight. Both the original 12.5 and the interest."

I didn't say anything. I just leveled him with a look. I'd heard all of this from him before. Randy was a good poker player. He just had a habit of getting a little over-excited and didn't know when to stop. He usually paid back his debts before the 50% interest stacked up so high. I didn't know why this time was different.

"You have the 5 grand to enter?"

His head moved like a bobblehead. "Yes, sir. I can use that and get the rest back for you. Tonight. I swear."

"And if you don't? What then? You'll still be collecting interest. That 5 would at least take you down some."

Now he looked more like a fish, with the way his mouth opened and closed. Hell, even his forehead was sweating enough that he could have just stepped out of the water.

Keith leaned on the bar. I turned just enough to give him permission to speak. I turned more when I saw the gleam in his eyes. My friend had an idea.

"Carlos got sick. He couldn't make it out tonight."

I tilted my head to the side, taking in his meaning, and thinking about it.

"Wh…who's Carlos?" Randy stuttered.

I tilted my head the other way, studying Randy more in-depth this time. "Didn't you once say that you wrestled in college?"

He licked his lips and wiped his sweaty hands on his pants. "Y… yah. I, uh, won state in high school and got a scholarship to UCLA. Why?"

The dark chuckle slipped out. I stood up straight again and took the tablet from Keith. He anticipated my move and was already handing it to me.

"I like you, Randy. Always have. But it wouldn't help my image any if it looked like I played favorites. We had a deal, you reneged on it. You are weeks late on paying off your debt to me." He opened his mouth to argue, but I cut him off with a hand. "I will give you two hours to win back my money. If you don't, I will help you win it another way. Do you understand?"

The color drained from his face. He probably already knew where I was going with this. He'd been around long enough. He was familiar with my various businesses. He'd placed bets on many of them, after all. He preferred cards, but a bet was a bet to a gambler.

"Okay." His answer was little more than a squeak. He scurried back to the table looking like a little rat.

Keith laughed as he watched me enter Randy's name in the docket for later tonight. "You know something I don't?"

"Yep." I handed him back the device. "Carlotta's gotten a lot better at hiding her tells. He hasn't played her in over a year. He's got one big surprise headed his way."

My friend tskd as he poured us both small shots of Coke on ice. "BoBo will be sad to hear it. You know how much he enjoys teaching lessons."

"I'm sure we'll find someone for him to teach soon. It's not like Randy is our only client. Nor will he stay gone for long, even after this."

"That's true."

I signaled for the dealer to come out and the game started. A couple of times a week we opened the room for poker games. Once a year, I hosted a tournament. The winning amount changed, based on how many people signed up. The buy-in was 5 grand. With our five players this year, the winnings were 25,000. We usually averaged 5-8 people playing. I could see why Randy wanted to win my money back this way.

Too bad it wouldn't work.

As the game progressed, I strolled through the room, visiting the players at the other tables. I made sure every player felt wanted, like they were a friend, and I was glad to see them. It helped encourage them to come back more often.

The first player to run out of chips left around the half-hour mark. The next person, fifteen minutes later. By an hour and a half, they were down to Carlotta and Randy. He was holding together pretty well. Their stacks were nearly even.

Randy wasn't so pale anymore. His confidence had returned. In his case, that wasn't always a good thing.

"I meet your 2,000, and I raise you another 100." Carlotta pushed her chips into the pile, her face blank of all expression. It had taken her a lot of work to overcome her need to bite her lip. Her nervous tick when she was trying to hide that she had a good hand. The stutter when bluffing hadn't been nearly as hard for her.

Randy studied her carefully, his eyes noting the way I circled around behind her. I purposely looked at my watch, as though checking the time.

He swiftly pushed all of his chips into the pile.

"I'm all in, call." Randy worked to keep his voice steady.

I moved to stand along the side of the wall with Keith. "He was doing so good too."

"His nerves get him every time. You did that on purpose, didn't you?"

I shrugged. "We needed to fill that slot."

"I'd have done it."

"I know you would have. And you would have wiped the floor with him. But…" I looked around carefully before lowering my voice further. "That's the one Carlos was going to take a fall for."

"Right, I forgot about that. Are we telling Randy that tidbit?"

I scoffed. "Do you really think we need to?"

Keith grinned and shook his head. "Nope."

"Full house, Kings and Queens." Randy laid his cards down proudly.

Keith whistled. "You might need me after all."

"Wait for it…." I sang softly. I was probably the only person who could still read Carlotta.

"Wow, that is one beautiful hand, Randy. Congrats." Carlotta said meaningfully.

Randy stood to grab all of his winnings, his grinning mouth open, probably to say thank you.

"But…" Carlotta flipped her cards over one at a time. Randy slowly sank back into his chair, defeated. "Royal flush. All hearts,"

"No," Randy whispered. He looked up as Keith stepped over and patted his shoulder roughly. "No." Randy shook his head, obviously in denial of what was about to happen.

With a little help from Keith, he walked out of the room. Not one person in there blinked an eye or even watched them. They didn't care. They were too focused on their own games and winnings. And losings.

Twenty minutes later, I walked into the much larger portion of my basement. This one was filled nearly to the brim with people. In the middle was a raised platform, with a net around it. Off to the side sat a small, curved bar, but this one was not for drinks – that one was on the opposite side and only served bottled beer. This was where the money was kept for bets. Rebecca sat on a stool behind it, collecting the money and tracking who bet what, on her company tablet. Two very large guards stood on either side of the bar ends. One of them was BoBo. Outside of them, guards were stationed all around the walls, keeping an eye on things.

"What's the score?" I asked Rebecca.

She swiped her finger along the tablet a few times before answering. "The first two shows are averaging around 50 in bets. The last is closer to 30. Many were hesitant to bet against your new guy. They think you are going to surprise them with something tonight. Are you?" She finally lifted her head up to look at me, her black bob cut brushing her nose.

I grinned. "Yes, but not the way they are thinking. It'll be a good show, that's for sure."

With one succinct nod, Rebecca waved for the next person to step up. I moved away, heading towards the back. My way was blocked by two large Russians before I made it halfway there.

"You made change. I not agree to any change."

I sighed and turned to face the thick accent behind me. I plastered my business grin on before greeting him.

"Ivan." I made a show of looking around him. "Where is your beautiful girlfriend? I saw you both inside the club earlier, you seemed to be enjoying yourself."

"Do not change subject. Why you change fighter?"

"Carlos caught the flu." I raised my arms to the side like I was helpless. "I had to replace him for the night."

"We had deal."

"And we still do. This man is not a fighter. He is a gambler."

The corners of Ivan's lips ticked upward, like they wanted to smile, but I was pretty sure that was as far up as his cheek muscles could go.

"You collect debt tonight?"

I winked at him and walked away. The laughter of his men followed me.

I didn't often run fixed fights, but when the Russians asked nicely, I granted them the favor. Their version of "nicely" fit very well into my bank account. Carlos got most of that since he was the one who had to get beat. I would still let him keep tonight's money though.

Randy would be lucky if he still had 4 working limbs by the end of the night.

The first two fights ran smoothly. The first lasted twenty minutes, the second five. As soon as Randy and his opponent walked out, the under-the-table bets blew up. The official betting table closed a few minutes before each fight. We allowed the other ones to continue, especially since each of those bookies had to pay a cut of their winnings in order to be invited each time.

Once again, Randy wouldn't need to know about those.

Keith had to help the visibly shaking man through the ropes, and then pushed him when he froze, one leg still hanging out. Randy had finally gotten a good look at who he was fighting. A Russian hitman, a pro.

He was far above 6 feet, his arms nearly as wide as his head. And more ink on him than skin. He was bald, but not shiny, as the ink all over his dome kept the shine off. I didn't know which scared Randy more, the mean mug on his face, or the wicked-looking scar running from his ear, down and across his neck.

I never asked Ivan why they wanted the fixed fights. I always assumed it was to show what they were capable of. It was only ever against one of my own fighters anyway.

The crowd laughed as Randy tried to straighten himself up. He closed his eyes in his corner, and I watched as he worked to center himself. It worked pretty good too. By the time the referee blew his whistle, Randy seemed more focused and less scared.

He did well for the first few minutes, even managing to knock the Russian's legs out from under him. The Russian pinned Randy twice before he realized Randy knew how to get out of that just fine. Not long after that though, the Russian learned that Randy only knew how to wrestle. Boxing and Martial Arts were not in his wheelhouse. All in all, Randy lasted just over 10 minutes.

Keith helped Randy out of the ring after the fight, only supporting about half his weight. After the place had cleared out, and all the winnings had been paid, Randy limped back out to me, his face already turning all sorts of colors. I was sure his chest looked worse.

"Are we even now?" He rasped.

"Close." I lifted my beer; grateful the night was finally ending.

Randy looked like he might need the drink more than me. "How much?"

"10. If not paid by the end of the week, then 13. I'll lower the interest for this week only, since you put up a good fight. You know how this works though, Randy."

If I wasn't mistaken, there were tears forming in his eyes. "I'll have the 10 here. I promise." And with that, he limped out the door.

"He lasted longer than I thought he would." Keith stepped behind the small bar and opened the minifridge, he pulled out a beer for himself.

"That he did. And because of that, more people bet on him."

"And let me guess," he popped the top off and took a long drink, "you had bets against him."

I chuckled and started our trek out, knowing he would follow. "You know me well, old friend."

Chapter 3

Fiona

Thursday evening, I sank into the waiting Uber after work, wanting nothing more than to soak in a hot bath, drink some wine, and fall asleep right there.

It had been a long week at work, and we weren't quite through it yet. Sunday, after the house was emptied and the storage unit locked up tight, Randy and I met Dad for dinner at his new place.

I loved hearing about Dad's new friends, and the different activities available for him. For someone who had always looked down on nursing and retirement homes, he seemed really happy there.

Dad usually ate in the cafeteria with his friends, or ordered his food delivered to his room if he was too tired. Thankfully he had a small kitchen in his apartment, so I was able to make us dinner in private.

All in all, it was a good visit. Randy made a few comments about how nice the place was, he did that nearly every time he was there.

Which, honestly, wasn't all that often. I ignored him this time though. Yes, this was nicer than expected - we'd heard some rumors about cheap and crappy places before. Yes, that meant it was more expensive. But it was worth it for our Dad to have the care he needed, and to be safe. It was a good fit for him, too.

I had dinner with Dad again on Monday, in the cafeteria - I was curious to see if it was as edible as he said it was. One bite and I was tempted to go back every day just so I didn't have to cook. I had also promised Dad that I would tell him how my first day as a Junior partner went. I decided to go in person, instead of calling, because it felt so good to see his big smile so often again. It was such a change from the past. It made me feel good to see pride in those eyes again, instead of all that regret and shame.

It felt like I finally had my Dad back.

At first, it didn't sound like my role at work would be all that different from before. Chris, the Junior partner I used to work under, had delegated a lot of things to me anyway (which probably helped me get noticed in the first place). But overseeing so many people and their tasks, on top of my own, was exhausting. I also had to meet with more clients than before. And much to my horror, I had to help bring in clients as well. I wasn't really known for my people skills. I was a stereotypical computer geek, all the way down to the introvert inside.

Not long after we merged into the downtown traffic, my phone buzzed. Thinking it was Katia, I picked it up. I really wished it had been Katia messaging me.

Randy: Can you swing by? Tonight.

I dramatically whimpered. Out loud. Then stomped my feet on the ground like a toddler.

"Everything all, sweetheart?" The cute older lady, Judy, driving me asked.

I sighed. "Yeah, just my brother. Mind if I change our destination?"

"Sure. Don't bother me none. Although you look like you should just go home and get some rest."

With a smirk, I nodded my agreement. "If only, Judy. If only." I gave her his address, which was going to cost me more to get there, then settled back in.

Me: On my way. You're lucky I was still in the Uber.
Randy: Thanks, sis. You're the best.

I was the best, huh? Guess I knew what he needed then. I just gave him 5,000 a few days ago though. He never needed money so soon like this. Maybe this was about something else. Had to be.

It took nearly an hour to get there when it would have only taken me half that to get to my place. When I got to his floor, I used my key to let myself in. I was met with nothing but darkness.

Weird.

I flipped the light next to the door as I called for him. "Randy?"

When he didn't respond by the time I hung my purse on the coat hangers nearby and slid out of my shoes, I went on a search for him.

"Randy?" I called again, entering his living room. I reached for the lamp behind the couch and flipped it on.

"Hey, sis."

I screeched, not having seen him lying on the couch. I cursed when I got a look at his face.

"Yeah, I know. It looks bad. I'd like to say it looks worse than it is, but to be honest, it's just the opposite. Since you can only see my face." That was true, the rest of him was in sweats.

"What the hell happened?" I screamed as I walked toward his very small kitchen and opened the fridge. I grabbed a couple beers. I had a feeling I was going to need something stronger than the wine I had at home.

"What do you think?" He groaned as he pushed into a sitting position, accepting the bottle I set in front of him, the top already off.

I sighed and sank onto the coffee table in front of him. "I gave you the money though."

He nodded and looked like he was about to cry. All this time, all these debts, and not once had he cried.

"It wasn't really the amount I owed. But there was a high-stakes game, and I knew all the players there. The winnings would have been just enough to pay off my debt. Dillan wasn't going to let me at first, but then he agreed to let me try." Randy gulped. "The 5,000 was the entry fee."

"I take it you didn't win, and they taught you a lesson." And here I thought I couldn't get any more tired than I already was.

"Yes and no. I'm sure that was part of it. I came really close to winning. The last two of us were nearly tied in chips. But Dillan had given me a 2-hour limit. I was running out of time. I had a royal full house. I thought I was in the clear. I swear."

He always did.

"You went all in?"

"How in the hell was I supposed to know she would get a royal flush? Do you know how rare those are?"

I rubbed my forehead with another sigh. I just wanted to sleep. Eat and sleep. And forget. "Then what happened?" Get to the point. Get to where you ask me for the leftovers.

Randy licked his lips and grimaced, probably from the giant swollen cut on his lip. "Dillan doesn't just do poker in the back of his club. He also runs an underground fighting ring."

I cursed, softly this time.

"Yeah. I about peed my pants when he told me that I'd have to fight to pay back my debt. Those guys can be ruthless."

I needed to move around. I couldn't just sit there. Nor did I want him to see my face when he dropped the bomb he was holding. I was too tired and worn out to keep control tonight. So, I stood up and started fixing us a couple sandwiches. At least he kept a well-stocked fridge.

"Did it work? Did it pay off your debt?" Did I sound as defeated as I felt? Utterly dead inside.

"Most of it." He cleared his throat. "I have until Friday to pay back the rest before the next 50% hits."

Ah, interest, my nemesis. "Want me to hack into his system and leave a virus? He'll never know who it was. Might buy you some time."

Randy snorted but didn't say anything. We both knew I would never do that. I mean, I could. I caught hackers for a living. I hacked into many places to test our clients' security systems. Hell, I hacked into a financial company this morning, right in front of them, just to make a point. Kurt, the Senior partner in the room, nearly had a heart attack when I pulled that out of my rear. To his credit, he supported me and let me run with it. We now had a new client, and I got a free lunch out of it.

All was quiet until I set the overly stuffed sandwiches, baby carrots, broccoli, and ranch, on the table. Randy was a crap eater, I had to force the veggies on him every chance I got. He only had these things because I frequently hacked into his grocery delivery order and added them. Which was also why there was a package of cookies sitting on the counter, right where he could see them. He knew the rules, which was why he picked up a carrot first.

We ate in silence, and I replaced our beers with bottles of water. It wasn't until I was nearly done that I brought up the subject.

"How much?"

"10."

I set the last of my sandwich down and leaned back. That was just about what I had left in my savings account. The one I had set aside to buy me my own car soon. I wanted to pay at least half down, making lower monthly payments.

It only took one look at my bruised and broken brother to make up my mind.

"This is the last time." It would have to be. I couldn't keep doing this. Financially or mentally.

He nodded quickly. "I swear."

"Where is Dillan? Where can I find him?"

That got Randy's attention real fast, his eyes had already started wandering over to the cookies. "What? Why?"

I snorted. "Because I'm going to make sure he gets the money this time. That's why."

"He will, honest. I don't wanna fight again, or have BoBo hunt me down."

I snorted, choking back a laugh. "Who's BoBo?"

"The guy they send to make you pay."

Yuck. "Randy, I love you, and you know I want to help you. But the only way that is going to happen is if you let me do it this time. I don't want you going anywhere near that place again."

He looked like he wanted to argue, but wisely chose not to. He gruffly gave me the instructions on how to find Dillan. I'd never heard of *Club Indecent*, but considering I wasn't really a club person, that wasn't surprising.

 As he spoke, I traded our now empty plates for the pack of cookies. Randy waited until I grabbed one before he did. Somebody was playing nice tonight.

"Have you seen a doctor yet?"

"Yeah, a couple of bruised ribs but at least nothing is broken."

I snorted. "Except your face. What about work?"

"I told them I caught covid again, which will give me about a week to get better."

"You didn't need to show them a test, prove it?"

He waved it away before grabbing a second cookie. "Nah, they don't really need it anymore. No covid leave either, it's just regular sick leave. I don't use much of that anyway, so I have the time."

I sighed and leaned on the table. The late hour was really beginning to weigh on me. I mean it was nearly nine… yeah, I heard that too. Not even 30 yet and I wanted to be unconscious by 9pm. Nor did I know the name of one of the hottest clubs in LA.

I needed a life.

Outside of the virtual world.

Randy looked at the time on his watch and pushed himself to stand up. He swayed a bit, so I jumped up to help. He didn't want it, but I did it anyway.

"Are sure you're alright? Do you want me to stay here tonight?"

He huffed and leaned over to kiss the side of my head, since we were close to the same height. "I'm fine, Pixie. I just sat in one position for too long."

I frowned, more at the nickname than anything else. Only Dad called me that, he was the only one I let get away with it. And Randy knew that.

I locked the door behind me after I left and sighed. I really hoped he learned his lesson this time. I wasn't even mad at Dillan for making my brother fight. Maybe if something had been broken, or he had been permanently injured, I would feel differently. But no. I was forever optimistic, and that would be my downfall.

I barely made it home and to my bed before I was out cold.

The next day, I was sitting at my desk, elbow deep in digital paperwork, when there was a knock on my door.

"Come in." I hollered absentmindedly.

My door opened and a deep, cheerful voice echoed around the room.

"It's been a week, and you haven't decorated yet?"

My head snapped up, finally realizing someone was in my office. I laughed softly and stretched my fingers.

"Haven't had the time. What's up, Chris?"

Chris was five years older, and only about an inch taller than me, with a full head of blonde hair. He looked like the typical Cali boy. But the nerd style, not the surfer. Up until a week ago, he was my boss. Now we were on the same level. It was still kind of weird.

"Nothing, just wanted to come see how you were settling into your new position, and to see if you wanted to get lunch. I didn't get a chance to congratulate you before they moved you up to this floor."

I rolled my eyes at him. "I'm like, 20 feet away. You make it sound like another building entirely."

We didn't exactly see each other all that often before anyway. Our firm took up exactly four floors in the building. The first two were filled with a variety of staff from security to cyber analysts, my old job. The third was for the junior partners and the conference rooms. And the fourth was the senior partners and their secretaries.

Chris stuck his hands in his pockets, acting shy. I knew he did that on occasion, I just didn't know why he would with me. He never had before. But then, I had been his underling for the last three years, up until a week ago.

"True, but with how busy it gets, it feels like it sometimes. So, what do you say, Chinese?"

I crinkled my eyes in confusion. "Chinese what?"

Chris both rolled his eyes and shook his head. "Lunch. I just asked you to go to lunch with me…"

My eyes widened and shot to the clock on the wall. Sure enough, it was nearly 1pm. I cursed and jumped up. Belatedly remembering I was in a skirt that had to be straightened out, as did my white button-up blouse. I straightened out the collar, fixed the buttons I loosened earlier, and retucked in my shirt. From the corner of my eye, I could have sworn I saw Chris blush and adjust his pants. When I looked up though, he was just standing there with his hands in his pocket, acting shy again. I was probably seeing things.

"I have to get to the bank during my lunch, and they aren't exactly close. Raincheck?"

Chris opened his mouth to answer, but nothing came out. He settled for clearing his throat and nodding.

"Great." I bent down a bit and unlocked the bottom drawer of my desk, trading out my laptop for my hidden purse.

Chris didn't move an inch.

"You okay?" I asked, walking towards the door.

"Ya huh." He spun on his heel and followed me out, signaling he'd hold it and close it for me.

We walked, in what felt like an awkward silence that I didn't understand, all the way to the elevator. Quite a few people in the building we used were coming and going, so that helped a bit. As soon as we stepped out onto the street Chris finally spoke.

"Do you want a ride? Maybe we could grab something along the way."

If this were any other errand, I would accept. But the last thing I needed were questions on why I was drawing out so much money.

"No, I'm good. I might just walk. The weather is nice right now, and traffic is horrible around here anyway." I laughed softly. "This will probably be faster."

"True. Alright. I'll see you later."

He leaned in and kissed my cheek, which was new, and sweet. I kissed his back. With one more wave, I turned and walked away from him. I did my best not to lose my balance in my heels, since I felt his eyes on me still. I hadn't planned on walking, but it was too late to order an Uber, and I couldn't exactly say I would rather take a cab. He knew I hated cabs. I may or may not have gone on a rant about one at the beginning of a team meeting a few years ago. After that, it had been a long-running joke.

By the time I made it to the bank, nearly 20 minutes later, I wanted to burn every pair of high-heeled shoes in the world and murder whoever invented them. I was so tired that I didn't even complain when they said I would have to sit and wait for someone to come talk to me, since I was pulling out so much money.

I gave them my preplanned spiel about helping pay for my Dad's nursing home, but I was trying to do it without him knowing. The plan was to deposit it into his bank account with his next retirement check. Yes, the amount was much larger, but he was getting older. As long as he saw a deposit slip, he was fine. He wouldn't look at the amount. The banker thought it was an odd idea but hoped it worked out for me.

So. Did. I.

This time, I ordered an Uber to drive me back across town. My hour was just about up. And, thankfully, Chris was nowhere around.

I stayed a little later that night - my nerves made me want to put off going - than I normally would. Around 7 pm, the last straggler left, along with the last of the three senior partners, Gary. I had no more reasons to stay, nor did I want anyone to think I was up to anything fishy.

I ordered another Uber and sat in the lobby to wait. My phone rang not long after my butt hit the chair. With a smile, happy for the distraction, I answered Katia's call.

"Hey, Kat. What's up?"

"Hey, yourself. How was your first official week as a partner?"

I smiled, feeling more at ease now. "Exhausting. But rewarding. I absolutely love it."

"Awesome. Now, tell me… what was the best part?"

I laughed. "Easy. Hacking into a brokerage firm with the CEO sitting across the table from me. They thought they already had the best cyber security. I proved them wrong."

Katia cackled from the other side. "I still say you would have been rolling in the dough by now if you wanted to go rogue."

"Eh. Maybe, but that is not me. Honest to a fault."

Seriously, I hacked into a school bully's TikTok account once, fully planning on messing with him. It was payback for him being a royal turd to my girl. But… I chickened out. It wasn't that I was afraid of getting caught, I knew I wouldn't. It was more just the idea of lying about it that bothered me. It was wrong. Besides, then I would have been the bully. The kid was a butthead, but that didn't mean I had a right to be one as well.

"Psh, honesty is not a fault. It's an honorable trait. Don't believe me, check your position at work. No way they would have promoted you if you weren't as awesome as you are."

I giggled. "Thanks, I appreciate it. Anything new with you?"

"Not really. I'm pregnant again." She let that bomb out in a sigh. "Two months already, too."

My jaw dropped. "I thought you guys decided you were done?"

Katia snorted. "I decided, Andy decided. But his sperm and my egg did not. We've been double-teaming the protection, but…" she sighed, "Andy's sperm is just as persistent as him."

I couldn't help but laugh at the badly hidden pride in her voice.

Andy had a thing for Katia in high school. She always said no. Then, we all ended up at the same college - she had gotten accepted to 2 schools, only one came with a full-ride scholarship, the backup one - we just didn't know he was there until Junior year. He had done a lot of growing up and filling out. Gone was the gangly dweeb, and in came the Adonis. Well, physically anyway. Andy was still a dweeb, in my opinion. Katia still made him work for it, and the minute he had it, he refused to let it go. The man even proposed on their one-month anniversary.

"Well, congrats. Maybe you'll get a son out of it this time. I'm sure Andy would love that." My phone beeped and I quickly moved it away from my ear so I could check it. Sure enough, my ride was here.

"Believe it or not, he wants another daughter."

I walked out of the building and looked for my ride. As soon as I stepped out, the college kid waved me over.

"That is both surprising and sweet."

"Yeah." She sighed dreamily. "So, you wanna come over for dinner tonight?"

"Where to ma'am?" The driver asked as he held the back door open for me. It was odd, but alright.

"I put the location in on the app."

"Cool."

I huffed in amusement at his childish response as he closed the door.

"Fi! You listening?" Katia called, again apparently.

"Sorry, my ride just got here. What were you saying?"

"Good timing, tell him to bring you here. You can come and have dinner with us. You haven't seen the girls in ages."

"Two weeks is not ages, and I wish I could. But I have to do a few things tonight, then I'm crashing. Hard." Maybe after that hot bubble bath and glass of wine I didn't get last night.

The driver closed his door and pulled up the app for the location. "Sweet, *Club Indecent*. I was there last week. That place is awesome." He looked at me warily through the mirror. "You wanna stop at home to change first. I mean you look good the way you are right now, but those aren't really club clothes, ya know?"

"What did he say about a club?" Katia broke in.

I cursed silently to myself. "No but thank you. I have a meeting there. I'm not going for fun." I told the driver, then gave my attention back to Katia. "It's nothing, Kat. Just something I have to take care of."

I wasn't the one cursing this time. "He did it again, didn't he? Wait, but why would you be going to a club? I'm confused."

I sighed. "It's kind of a long story."

She snorted. "It always is with Randy."

"Kat…"

I could almost hear the eye roll. "I know, I know, I know. He's your only brother. Someone has to look out for him, yada, yada, yada. I'll save both of us the time and stress and just jump to the please be careful part."

"I will. It's going to be quick. In and out."

Yeah… it was so not going to be a quick in. And from the looks of things, I doubted it would be a quick out too. The line to get in was ridiculous. And after seeing the way all the other women were dressed, I understood why the driver said I should change.

I was way more covered than them.

I had no desire to wait in line, my feet were ready to sue for a divorce. Taking my chances, I cut to the front and approached the bouncer handling the entry fee. Seeing me jump ahead like that, another bouncer - both of them were dressed in black tactical pants and black t-shirts that said *Indecent* in the top left corner - came to stand next to him. I didn't think I looked like a threat, but who knew what kind of threats they got in a place like this. The only threat I posed was definitely not of a physical nature.

"Hi." I smiled self-consciously. They lifted an eyebrow and took in my attire. "I, uh, need to speak with Dillan."

They looked at each other, and then back at me. They were both frowning now.

"Do either of you know how to speak in words, or just in the ape version of sign language?"

Someone behind me snorted into laughter. I was tired and I didn't want to be there. I also might have a small issue with my mouth when I got this tired. Or when I was nervous. Again, people were not my thing.

The main bouncer smirked. "You need to wait in line, Ma'am."

"But I really don't want to. Especially since I just need to drop something off and get out of here. I mean, seriously, do I look like the normal type of person who goes out to a club on a Friday night." I spun to the girls right behind me. "No offense."

The one closer shrugged. "None taken. You do you, honey."

I grinned. "Thank you." My grin slid back off when I turned back to the behemoths. "Trust me, Dillan is going to want to see me."

The big man spoke this time. "Every woman says that." His voice was far from soothing in that deep scratchy kind of way. It irked me even more.

I waved at the building and the large crowd. "Judging by the popularity of his club, I wouldn't doubt that. Women love a man who can provide. Now, I am going to say this one more time, as I am trying to do this without spreading all of Dillan's business to the gossipy world. I am here to drop something off. Something he has been waiting for. *Randy* would have come himself, but he seems to… not be himself lately. He's been confined to his apartment the last few days."

The large one's face changed slightly when I emphasized Randy's name. It wasn't much, but I was hoping it was recognition. My suspicions were confirmed when his eyes dropped to the purse I held tightly to my stomach. It was a cross-body strap, but one could never be too careful. Carrying 10,000 dollars in cash around was wearing on my nerves. Adding more figurative weight to my already weary shoulders.

"From Randy, you say?"

"Yes. Now can I see Dillan, or not?"

"Let her go, BoBo." The main bouncer said softly. "She's right, Dillan will want to see her."

I giggled. "You're BoBo?"

The large man eyed me. "What's it to you?"

I shrugged, trying to play it cool. That name was hilarious, but I didn't think he was the kind to like being laughed at.

"Nothing really. Randy told me about you. The name stuck out."

The main bouncer choked on the laugh he was trying to hide. BoBo smacked him on the shoulder then stepped to the door.

"Go wait at the bar, someone will tell you where to go from there." He grumped at me as he pushed the door open.

I stepped through quickly, before he could change his mind. I turned to thank him, but the door was already closing.

I had to take a minute to steady myself as I took in a *very* unfamiliar environment. There were a few times growing up, when I wondered what it would be like to be a normal girl and go to clubs with my friends.

Judging by what I saw, I hadn't missed much. Good to know.

I made my way to the bar to wait, and decided I could use something to help settle my nerves. I nearly changed my mind when I saw how busy it was. I tried to wave the bartender down, for both a drink, and directions on where to go from there, but that was not an easy thing to do.

It took ages, but I eventually made my way through the crowds and leaned halfway over the bar. I finally got the guy's attention when, instead of a drink, I asked "where's Dillan?"

He seemed a bit confused with how forward I was about it. I guess it came off like I knew the man, which I didn't. He could be the bartender I was already talking to for all I knew.

"Uh." The man looked around the club, still a bit off, then smiled in relief. "He's at his booth. Follow the room around to your left. It's the only booth roped off."

I gave him a thumbs up, because I was already getting tired of yelling over the music and pushed back through the crowd. They were happier to let me out than they were to let me in. I was happy to know that it wasn't as crowded walking around the edges of the club.

For the first time that night, or in a long time actually, I had no words. The first moment I laid eyes on Dillan, the ability to even formulate a thought flew out of my mind. Between his perfectly proportioned muscles, the wavy black hair cut to just above his ears, the dimple on his right cheek, and the tilt of those thick lips, I knew I was screwed.

Then I noticed the arm he had over the blonde skank. I was grateful for her presence because it reminded me what kind of man I was dealing with. It cleared up the fog in my brain post-haste.

Chapter 4

Dillan

Instead of walking around the club tonight, I decided to just sit back in my booth. We didn't have anything extra going on, so I could afford a little downtime. The music and noise of the crowd were wearing on my nerves though, so I doubted I would last long before heading up to my office.

I kind of wished we had the basement opened, but we usually avoided that on Fridays and Saturdays. It was too obvious, too predictable.

About five minutes after I sat down, Bunny slid in next to me. I put my arm around her out of habit, letting her move in close.

"What's going on? Everything alright?" I asked her.

"Can't a girl just want some of your attention?" She batted her fake eyelashes at me, giving me that seductive smile she gave to the customers on a regular basis.

"You know the rules, Bunny." I lightly reprimanded her, stopping her hand from unbuttoning my shirt.

She growled softly in frustration and dropped the act. "Fine. We might have another cop on our hands."

I pulled my head back a bit. "Might?"

"Yeah, BoBo wasn't sure. A chick was at the door saying you wanted to meet with her. Said something about Randy being confined to his apartment and she came in his place."

That did sound odd. "Is she still outside?"

"No, she threatened to broadcast your hidden stuff in front of everyone, so BoBo let her in. She's over at the bar."

"What does BoBo think?" He was a good judge of character, so I trusted him. He was my head of security for a reason.

Bunny shrugged. "She kind of threw him for a loop. He says she is pretty but dressed like she has a stick up her butt, and yet has a mouth on her. So, he thought maybe Randy got picked up for something and was on house arrest. Maybe he sold you out. He told her to wait at the bar for further instructions."

I doubted Randy had done anything to get picked up. I always vetted potential clients before loaning them money. But there were those other cops the other day. Could they have seen Randy at some point and picked him up? Were they trying to use him to get close to me?

I was pulled from my thoughts when Bunny cursed. "Kent just pointed you out to her. Idiot."

"He is still learning how to read people. And if she threw BoBo for a loop, I'm sure she did a number on Kent."

"True. You want me to go, give you two a minute?"

"No, not yet. Let's see how this plays out."

I watched as the woman grew closer. I couldn't see much of her in the dark, not until she was directly in front of my table. I kept it roped off just to remind the drunk idiots that this booth was off-limits. It was in a prime spot to see everywhere in the room.

I watched with pride as she took me in. She was gorgeous and had been wreaking havoc with my staff in the short time she'd been there. And yet, one look at me, and her reign ended.

Until her eyes fell onto Bunny, and then the change in her demeanor was obvious.

I was a little torn. Part of me wished I had told Bunny to leave, so I could have seen how long my effect on her would last. But I also really wanted to hear what she had to say. To see first-hand how she messed with my men.

"Can I help you?" Bunny asked, her voice irritating me for the first time.

The woman rolled her eyes and scoffed. "I doubt you could help anyone, honey. Unless it was to take their pants off and take all their money."

I lifted my free hand and put a fist over my mouth, trying to cover my laugh with a cough. Bunny was not amused by either of us.

I patted Bunny's shoulder gently. "Get back to work. I'll talk to you later."

With a disgruntled grunt, Bunny slid out of my booth. I saw the way she moved and knew she was going to try and hip-check the woman. The woman wasn't stupid though, she stepped to her right, just in time. It caused Bunny to go off balance just a bit. I bit back the laugh again.

This woman was delightful. And just what I needed to spice up a boring night.

Once Bunny was gone, the woman looked back at me. Her hazel eyes hypnotized me, as did the small opening made by her top with two buttons being undone. It provided just enough of a tease that it held my interest. I wished she wasn't wearing the white undershirt, as these lights would have shone straight through, giving me what I was sure was the real best view in the house.

When my eyes met hers again, she gave me the "I dare you" look. What this unknown woman didn't realize was that I lived for a challenge. And this was definitely a challenge I would accept.

"I heard you were looking for me." I said it just soft enough that she had to move closer.

"Are you Dillan?" She hollered back.

I slid an inch further into the booth and patted the seat. "Why don't you sit down? That way we don't have to yell like barbarians."

She fought the smirk, but slid in, holding her purse close to her chest. Sadly, that meant it hid her tempting body from me. I would have to see what I could do about that.

"Are you Dillan?" She repeated, her voice much softer, and less edgy. A thin layer of exhaustion coated her words now.

Unable to help myself, I put my arm over the back of the booth, right behind her. She turned just a smidge, facing me, moving away from my arm at the same time.

"You have me at a disadvantage, beautiful. You know me, but I don't know you."

"You don't need to. I just need to deliver something to you."

"Yes, for Randy. What is it that he has sent you to do for him?"

She made an adorable sound of derision. "He didn't send me. I forced him to tell me how to find you. It was a lot easier to do since he isn't exactly in all that great of shape. Thanks for that by the way. I hope he learns his lesson this time."

I moved my arm back just a bit, starting to get a little more of the picture. I may be a lot of things, but a homewrecker was not one of them.

"Randy sent his girlfriend to pay off his debt?" He was more of a coward than I thought.

The beauty by my side cringed. "Hell, no. I am not his girlfriend. Ew."

I chuckled and moved my arm back, sliding a tad bit closer at the same time. She was grossed out enough by the comment that she didn't seem to notice. I took advantage of that fact and went a step further. I lightly began to brush my fingers through her long brown hair. It felt better than imagined.

"Then who are you?"

She grimaced again. "His sister."

"Ah. So, the little brother got himself in too deep this time and went running to big sis to rescue him. Must have been quite the shock for you." The look on her face was telling. It was subtle, but the small grimace behind the eyes was there. "Or was it not a surprise?"

She blew out a breath and melted just a bit as my fingers slowly started working closer to the back of her neck. Somebody needed a good massage.

"Not a surprise, nor am I the older one. Not physically anyway."

My hand froze. "Randy went to his little sister to bail him out? How bad was he hurt to do that?" Pathetic. That's what Randy was. Pathetic.

She turned her head away, facing another direction. This enigma of a woman felt guilty for something.

I lifted my right hand and stroked the edge of her jaw with my knuckle, bringing her face back to me. Her breath quickened as she filled my silent request. I had a feeling the challenge wasn't going to be between her and me. More like her against herself. She was stubborn, that much was obvious from the way she stormed in here. There was a desire for more though.

For someone to really see her maybe?

"This isn't the first time you had to bail him out." I stroked her chin a few more times, then slowly dragged it down the middle of her neck. I would have dragged it down her chest next, lightly brushing her… but that dang purse was in the way. My movement brought her out of whatever stupor she had fallen into, and her strong facade was back.

She cleared her throat and straightened her back. She used one hand to pull the bottom of her skirt down, like she was making sure it hadn't come up when she moved. Oddly, the movement brought her a little closer to me. I didn't care if it was on purpose or not. Now there was barely an inch of air between our legs. One small move and I could have that chest next to mine.

When her eyes met mine again, she seemed a little surprised at how close we were suddenly. I grinned.

"Um, no. It's not." She was a bit breathless, which made my grin grow. She scowled at me for that, which didn't help me not smile at her. Even her scowl was sexy.

"No? So, you often have to hunt down those he owes and pay them off?"

She half-heartedly snorted. I was pretty sure she was suddenly feeling off her game tonight. Good.

"No, this is the first time since high school that I have personally paid off his debts. And that time was only because I stopped the guy from beating him to a pulp."

It was my turn to frown. "You've been paying off your older brother's debts since high school?" I was pretty sure our ages weren't that far off, which meant high school wasn't exactly yesterday.

"Sadly, yes. I didn't trust him this time, not after what happened the other day. He told me he only owed you 5,000, which I now know was a lie. I'm sorry he got hurt because of it, but I truly hope he learned from it - although I doubt it." She sighed sadly. "Look, can I just give this to you and call it a night? I literally came here from work and I'm tired."

I believed it. She looked tired. But not just from working all day. She needed the break from reality as much as I did. A change of pace.

Pushing the limits, I moved my right hand down to her knees and played with the rim of her skirt. Her eyes locked on mine, but she didn't say anything. Not verbally anyway. Her eyes lit on fire, begging me. I buckled to their beauty and slowly began sliding my hand between her legs, which parted slightly for me.

As my hand made its way further North, I leaned in and began kissing her jaw. "Are you sure I can't convince you to stay for a while. I know a great way to help you relax."

"N… no. I don't find clubs all that relaxing."

"Oddly enough, I was thinking the very same thing before you showed up. We can leave, go somewhere more private." I moved down her neck, which she graciously made available to me.

She gasped when my hand grazed right along the edges of her now. I licked the flames of her neck and nibbled on it. Suddenly, her legs slapped shut on my hand and she ripped her head back. I chuckled. She moved away from my lips, but my hand was still firmly held in place. Just to be a brat, I wiggled my fingers slightly and she tensed.

"I only came here to pay my brother's debt of 10 grand. That's all."

My grin turned a bit evil, and a slight whimper came out of her. This was the most fun I had had in quite some time. And we hadn't even made it to the good part yet.

"Oh, but sweetheart. His debt stopped being 10 grand when the clock struck 7."

"That's impossible. Randy said he had until Friday. Today is Friday." She cursed and shook her head, her eyes closed. "I can't get any more to you any time soon. And I know he doesn't have it. He barely makes enough to cover his own bills."

Since I was probably already slotted for a trip to hell when this life was over anyway, I thought I would try one more thing.

"I could always take that last 3 in trade."

"What do you mean? You don't even know what I do, let alone my name."

I chuckled and leaned in to kiss the other side of her jaw now. "I think you know what I mean."

Shock rippled through me a second later as a sharp sting ran across my cheek. I had not seen that one coming. She actually slapped me!

"Listen to me carefully, I will say this only once." She practically growled the words through her teeth, all the while pulling my hand away from where it was comfy and warm. "I. Am. Not. A. Hoe. You want to pay someone, go find the little tramp you just had all over you."

Any other man would have crawled into a hole to hide from the anger burning in her eyes. Not me. It made me want her more.

Without thinking about it. I pulled her head back with the hand still in her hair and met her half way. I roughly slammed my lips onto hers. The fight left her rather quickly after my tongue invaded her mouth, claiming her. It was only seconds later that her arms wrapped around my head, and her chest was pressed against mine. The purse having slipped to between our thighs.

We were both out of breath when I finally released her. I didn't let her move away though. I kept her locked in place and laid my forehead against hers.

"What the hell is your name?"

She huffed out a breathless laugh. "Fiona."

I groaned. "It's a fitting name for you. A beautiful name, for a beautiful woman."

She huffed again and tried to move away. I wasn't having it though. I kissed her again. Fiona whimpered when I moved away though.

"I am not calling you a hooker. I am asking you to spend one night with me. Not because I will ignore the last bit of interest, that will just be a favor I grant because you convinced me to. I want you to stay with me because I am entranced by your beauty, by your wit, and by this mouth." I pulled lightly on her bottom lip with my thumb, thinking about biting it.

"I...I don't..."

I rubbed the back of her head just hard enough to make her look up. "Stop over thinking it. It's one night. I doubt you have to work tomorrow, so what is the harm in releasing a bit of stress all night?"

"All night, huh? That's pretty presumptuous."

I chuckled at her and leaned down to her neck, biting it softly. "No, it's confidence."

Fiona moaned loudly into my ear, making my right hand drop back down to her legs. She refused to part them this time though.

"Not here."

The next bite was not so soft. Neither were her nails in the back of my neck as she held me in place. By the time either of us released the other, she was sporting quite the beauty mark.

"I have a small studio upstairs."

"Why? Do you take many women up there with you?" Her tone said she was offended by the thought of it, but there was a glimmer in her eyes.

I poked her in the side, causing her to break into a fit of giggles. Fiona was ticklish. That was going to be fun.

"No, smart mouth. I just can't wait long enough to take you somewhere else. I need to get my hands in you now."

"You mean on." Her eyes were still shining at me, her body already more relaxed than when she arrived.

Acting quickly, I roughly shoved my hand back up her skirt, forcing her legs apart. She gasped and her head fell back. My fingers didn't stop until two were all the way in, demonstrating my meaning.

"No. I didn't." I answered, leaning back down to that perfect neck.

Fiona didn't fight me. She was beyond that point of ability already. My lips trailed a path back up, where she was eagerly waiting to kiss me. We didn't stop this time until her body was shaking, dripping, and more relaxed than it probably had been in some time.

"I said not here." She groaned out, her forehead against my shoulder.

I petted the back of her head and laughed softly. "And I told you I couldn't wait. Do you think you can walk? Or do you need me to carry you to the elevator?"

"Hmmm. Normally I would say I could walk, but my feet are killing me. I don't know why I wore heels today."

I kissed her softly one more time, then signaled for her to exit the booth. As soon as I was standing next to her, I swiftly lifted her into my arms. She squeaked, either not expecting me to actually do it or because she wasn't ready. Either way, I laughed at her. She retaliated by hitting the back of my shoulder. I, of course, got back at her by pinching her butt. This went on until we reached a far corner of the room, where I had a hidden door.

Fiona was kind enough to reach down and twist the knob for me. I pushed the door open and then kicked it closed behind us. I did manage to put my thumb on the reader to call the elevator though.

"Ooh, fancy." Fiona teased me.

I smiled and kissed her head. "You can never be too careful with security."

"I agree completely."

"Really?"

She tipped her head up to look at me. "Yes. Security is something no one should ever put off or skimp on. All kinds of security are important. But there are many types that only seem safe on the outside. There is almost always a way into even the most secure areas."

I studied her intently, trying to put the pieces together. I didn't realize how hard I was looking at her, or for how long, until she started looking wary.

"What's wrong?" She whispered. "Why are you staring at me like that?"

The elevator doors slid open as I softened my look. "You are an enigma I am trying to figure out."

She scoffed uncomfortably and rolled her eyes, probably for something to do. "Not really. I am just a boring, run-of-the-mill person. There is literally nothing interesting about me."

I set her down in the elevator, only to pick her right back up again, her back against the wall this time. "I beg to differ. There are many, many things about you that I want to know. I find you to be a beautiful mystery. I would like to spend the night discovering each of them, but I don't think we will be doing very much talking."

A devious little grin took over her beautiful face. "Oh, yeah? And why is that? What else would we be doing all night? Sleeping? I really could use a nap."

She still held that purse strap tight in her hand, but at least it wasn't covering her chest anymore. I paved a path of kisses down the unbuttoned part of her shirt while I pressed into her down below. The whimper wasn't so quiet anymore. Her free hand moved to the back of my head, gripping my hair, and pushing my head down further.

"Shirt," I mumbled against her, not wanting to leave the smooth skin.

Fiona's purse hit the floor as she frantically began unbuttoning her shirt further. And like the good little girl she was, she pushed the top of her undershirt down on one side, so the only thing covering her was her bra. That wasn't a problem, I slid my tongue inside it. She pressed her head against the wall, trying to push her entire body closer to me.

I felt air hit more parts of my body as she took the initiative to relieve me of my own clothes. I laughed as she reached down and moved her own underwear for me. It was all the permission I needed. We both moaned loudly once I was in.

The echoes in that elevator only added to our intense need over the next few minutes. It was only after we finally started slowing down, our insatiable hunger for one another temporarily satiated, and just about all of our clothes on the floor now, that we noticed the elevator had stopped. The doors were closed, probably having already timed out after opening.

Regretfully, I disconnected our bodies. My only comfort was knowing I would be back in my new heaven shortly.

"Do you need me to carry you again?" I gave her a sarcastic smile.

She gave me a sickeningly sweet one back. "No, thank you. But I will take off these nightmare shoes first."

I laughed and bent down to take them off for her. Once they were off, I looked up in time to see her blush in full swing. I was beginning to get the feeling that it wasn't often that someone looked out for her. I could at least spend the night doing that.

Starting now.

Since I was already on my knees, and her left leg was still in my hand from when I lifted it to take her shoe off, I kissed her inner thigh. She shivered and fell against the wall for support. I made my way up, slowly placing her leg over my shoulder. It wasn't long before she had a handful of my hair again, and her echoes filled the elevator. The flavor of both our fluids on her body was the best thing I had ever tasted. I greedily cleaned up every last drop of it on her.

Eventually, I carried her out of the elevator and directly into the small studio apartment. I didn't put her down until she was laying on her back on my spare bed. I practically ripped that skirt off her, followed by any remaining articles of clothing on either of us. Then I spent the next hour getting to know her body inside and out.

We both passed out after that.

I woke up sometime later to someone shaking my shoulder. I blinked my eyes open, a bit confused at the woman sleeping soundly on my left arm, her back against my chest. It didn't take long for my mind, and body, to catch up.

My shoulder shook again, and I looked up into the amused eyes of my best friend. I raised my finger, asking for a minute. He nodded and stepped away. Very carefully, I slid my arm out from under her, chuckling softly at the pout on Fiona's beautifully swollen lips. I fixed the blanket over her, keeping her warm, and then grabbed my boxers.

"What's up? Everything alright downstairs?" I whispered, not wanting to wake her up.

Keith followed my lead. "It's fine. Bunny said some cop showed up and then you disappeared. Kent thought he saw you head for the elevator with a woman, so I thought I would check up here first. What happened?"

I scratched my jaw as I looked back at the sleeping angel in my bed. Although, I was beginning to think that angel thing didn't go all the way down deep in her. It felt more like a front for something else.

"She's not a cop, just a frustrated sister who has to keep bailing out her pathetic older brother."

"What?" His brows creased, obviously not following me.

"She's Randy's younger sister. She didn't trust him to give me the money and not gamble it away, so she came to find me herself."

"Then how did she end up in your bed?"

I shrugged. "She's hot and I couldn't resist. I also may have fibbed and moved the timeline for the interest up by a few hours."

He tskd sarcastically. "You paid her."

I pretended to be horrified. "I did not. Besides, that didn't work. It took a little more persuasion after that. She was battling herself. She wanted to come up here, but she is the complete opposite of Randy. She doesn't cave to what she wants, she maintains self-control." Mostly.

"Right…" Keith didn't believe me, understandably. "I guess all those clothes in the elevator were from both of you having self-control.

My face felt hot, making me wonder if I was blushing. "She has this effect on me. When I'm touching her, the rest of the world seems to disappear." I shrugged, trying to ignore the anxiety starting to creep in, the worry about why I felt such a need for her.

"Ya huh." He knew me well enough to know not to push. "Just how long are you planning on staying up here?"

"I convinced her to give me the night. Why?"

He tilted his head to the side. "I need to know how long to stay downstairs. I don't want to walk in on anything. It's bad enough that I know what you will be doing as soon as I turn my back."

I flipped him off. "Maybe I was planning on going back to sleep. She took a lot out of me."

His eyes flicked down, drawing mine. "You are locked and loaded. Those boxers aren't exactly hiding it. We both know where your mind has gone."

Denial was pointless, thanks to my body giving it away. "True. Keep an eye on the club for me." I walked away from him, already pushing my boxers down.

"Yep." He headed straight for the door, his back to me. Not that we hadn't seen either of each other's loaded guns enough times. We had shared this very same studio apartment after I got the loan to buy the building. We both saved money by living here.

I moved the blanket off Fiona, lifted her leg, and dove right in. Considering the door didn't close until after she screamed in the best way possible, and I had emptied completely again, I figured he had stayed to watch. That wouldn't be a first either. Kind of hard not to watch when one of you brought a girl home and you shared a room. More than once one of us got off to it. It was like watching live porn.

What was a first though, was my not realizing he was still there. I was pretty sure Fiona didn't either.

I didn't move away from her, only helped her roll to her back. Then I leaned down and kissed her softly.

"You woke me up."

I laughed as I dropped my forehead onto the pillow next to her head. "I did warn you it would be all night. And I'm just getting started."

Chapter 5

Fiona

I woke up to the sun shining brightly through the curtains. I lifted the blanket to pull it over my head, and discovered another body wrapped around me. I took a peek, because I could, and enjoyed the sight of the perfect specimen lying next to me. It was tempting to wake him the way he woke me all night. But this was also my chance to get out of there without a scene, or whatever. I didn't want to sit and listen to the "thanks, your debt is settled" speech.

My ego couldn't take that. Not after the best night of my life. A girl could definitely get used to the way he had taken care of me and devoured me.

Quietly, I slid out from under the octopus arms, detaching them from my various body parts. I walked around the room quietly, trying to find all of my clothes. I had to follow the trail back to the elevator to get them all. Which was when I realized it needed a fingerprint to even be called.

I was sure Dillan had an emergency stairwell around here somewhere, but my legs were even more tired now than they had been the night before.

With a smile, I remembered how sure he sounded about his security system last night. He didn't need to say it, his tone was enough. He thought his place was air tight.

I found my purse near the elevator door. I vaguely remembered dropping it in the elevator, after practically ripping it off me. I wondered if we kicked it out at some point. It was all kind of a blur.

I picked up my purse to search for my phone, praying the battery wasn't dead. My fingers froze though when they bumped into the very thick envelope full of cash. Talk about cold water being thrown over your head. The man not only bribed me to spend the night with him, but I had a sleepy memory of him talking with someone last night, saying something about changing the time of the interest increasing on purpose. I wasn't that deep of a sleeper. Which meant that Dillan not only bribed me, but he conned me.

He needed to learn a lesson. I wasn't getting back at a lil punk this time. I was teaching a grown man a life lesson about respecting the wishes of others.

Giggling to myself, I found my phone, and sighed in relief when I saw that it still had a little under half the battery left. I was glad I had charged it up during that last hour of work. Using my phone, I logged into his security system. I added my fingerprint to his database, so I could use the elevator. And, as payback, I deleted everyone else's. He would be trapped up here, with only the stairs to use, and no one would be able to use the elevator to get to him.

And to add insult to injury… I collected all of his clothes and threw them on the floor of the elevator. And I did mean ALL of his clothes. I found a few sets in the small dresser and quietly took them as well. I left the money on a two-seater table in the makeshift dining area, with a short note.

Consider the debt paid in full.
Enjoy the gift I left you.

With a triumphant grin on my face, I stepped into the elevator and pushed for it to go to the main floor. I had no desire to see any other part of his set up. While I rode down, I played around in his system a little more. It was decent, but not good enough. Not against me at any rate.

The elevator opened to the small lobby we had entered after exiting the main club area. There were two doors. One I recognized as the direction we had come from the night before, while the other was on the opposite side of the room. Taking a shot in the dark, I went for the new one.

Fresh warm air hit my face. A separate entrance and exit. That didn't surprise me in the least bit. I'd want a private entrance if I owned a club.

I walked around the building barefoot, preferring to carry my heels. I stopped dead when I came face to face with a large man sitting on the low wall dividing the alley from the entrance to the club.

"Morning," I mumbled, trying to walk around him without looking at him. It only became a walk of shame if people knew what you were doing. Or rather, *had* been doing.

"Afternoon, actually. You all had a late night." BoBo said, jumping off the wall and walking over to me.

I kept walking, hoping he'd get the hint. "Apparently so."

Either he didn't get the hint, or he ignored it. My bets were on the latter. "Why didn't you just tell me you were Randy's sister? I would have let you in."

I shrugged. "I'm not exactly a pro at this. I wasn't sure what I was and wasn't allowed to say."

When we reached the sidewalk, I moved to turn left. He grabbed my arm and pulled me right.

"My car is this way. I'll give you a lift home."

"Oh no. Really, I'm good. I already ordered an Uber anyway. I appreciate the thought though." Besides, I did not need any of Dillan's people knowing where I lived.

He scowled at me. "I will give you a ride home. Dillan would be upset if he thought I didn't make sure you got home safely."

I busted out in a laugh. "We both know what this was, don't pretend otherwise. I appreciate the offer. But I promise, if I got into that car with you, I would tell you the wrong address, get out, and then get into an Uber to take me somewhere else, go inside for a bit, then leave out a back door and into another Uber."

BoBo gave me a confused look, like he wasn't sure what to do with me. Thankfully, my Uber started approaching. I raised my arm to get the driver's attention as I continued talking.

"Let's save us both the trouble, and I'll take the one Uber now."

He scratched his head like the big ape he was, while I quickly jumped in the back seat of the Suburban. The housewife looking lady driving it gave me a big smile and greeted me. I hadn't realized I approved a carpool Uber until she made the next stop. Oh well. It would help save money. I was broke again after all.

As soon as I locked my front door behind me, I hightailed it to the shower. When I came out, my phone had a few missed calls, all from Katia. I called her back on speakerphone and set it on the bathroom counter.

"What's up? Everything alright?"

Katia cursed me out for a minute straight.

When she was finally done, I asked again. "Everything alright?"

"No, everything is not alright. Last I heard from you, you were going to some club called *Indecent*. That was more than 12 hours ago! You didn't answer my calls or messages. I did some research online about the club, and it is not a place you should be." She rambled on about all the crimes she believed were committed inside the doors of the club while I got dressed.

I was fully clothed, and teeth brushed by the time the tirade ended.

"You feel better now?" I asked, laughing at her. She verbally flipped me off.

"So, what happened? How did your *meeting* go?" I heard the incredulousness in her tone.

She already knew I lied, and I was too tired to keep it up. I told her everything. From Randy asking for the 5,000, to me leaving BoBo on the street.

"While I am shocked that you agreed to such a deal, I applaud your exit. That was awesome!"

I laughed with her. "I was a little surprised too, to be honest. Dillan had this weird effect on me. I was almost grateful that he gave me a reason to stay. Besides the fact that we both know I needed to get laid, a lot apparently. I just didn't want to move away from him. When I was with him, I kept forgetting about the rest of the world."

"I really wish you two could explore that more together."

I sighed. "Yeah, me too. But we both know what the odds are of him being involved with illegal activity, besides the whole poker and fighting ring thing. I can't get involved with stuff like that. Not only would it get me fired, but it would make the cops suspicious of me. It's not worth it. I just need to find someone else who is willing to worship this body like he did."

"I'm sure you will too. There are plenty of other fish in the sea. Now, why don't you come over and hang out? We can talk some more, and you can see your nieces."

"Ya huh. I will play with them, while you sneak off to play with Andy in your room together."

Katia laughed but didn't deny it.

I loved my best friend, so I grabbed another Uber and rode out to the Valley where they lived. I was going to have to cut back on my Uber trips soon. I wished LA had a better metro system.

Or that I had the money to buy a car.

After spending the rest of the day with Katia and her family, I let them twist my arm into staying the night. We all knew it would happen because it always did. My Dad lived in the Valley still and I was scheduled to visit him every Sunday. It was cheaper to just stay there. Plus, Andy offered to give me a ride to the nursing home.

I spent most of the day with my Dad and his friends. Randy arrived around 5 pm for dinner. Which was my cue to start cooking. Dad liked to offer ordering from the cafeteria, but I wanted these dinners to be family. And I wanted to take care of him whenever I had the chance. Thankfully, he relented.

Randy followed me to the kitchen, under the cover of offering to help.

"Did you do it?" He whispered, pulling out a baking pan.

I took the pan back to the cabinet and traded it for the right one. "Yes. It's done. And you better be done. I can't keep doing this, Randy."

He sighed and wrapped me in a hug from the side. "You're the best sister, you know that?"

I snorted. "Please, Randy. Please. For all of our sake, stop gambling."

He shuffled his feet back and kicked at the floor. "I'm trying. Really, I am."

I moved to put the noodles on to boil, I wasn't up for anything fancy, so they were getting spaghetti. "It would be easier to follow through if you avoided those places altogether. They will do everything they can to keep you under, just so they can make more off you."

"Nah, Dillan's not like that. Maybe some of the others, but Dillan is a straight shooter. He doesn't take advantage of people like that."

I couldn't help the half laugh/half snort that came out of me.

"No, really, Fi. You don't know him like I do."

I gave Randy the same smile I gave to my nieces when I was just appeasing them. "I'm sure you know him better than I do. I only met the man once. But sometimes that's all you need to know what kind of person someone is." I turned the burner on under the pan of ground beef to start frying before turning back to my brother.

"Randy, I love you. I want to help you. But you have to see that this is hurting me more than you. I'm the one that keeps making the sacrifices to bail you out. And then you went and lied to me about it all. This has to stop."

He pouted and shoved his hands in his pockets. "I know."

I sighed and gave him another hug, then pushed him out of the kitchen. I knew he felt bad for what happened, but I also knew it wasn't bad enough to make him stop. I worried about what would have to happen before he woke up to reality. I didn't tell him how I paid off his "interest" because there was no point. Besides, that was as much my fault as it was Dillan's.

Randy was kind enough to drive me home that night - it would at least get me closer to home - and smart enough not to ask when I was going to buy my own car. He'd asked that once before, and I told him I was saving up for one. He had to know that was the money I used to pay off his debt.

The next morning, I arrived at work at the same time as Chris. He held out a Styrofoam cup to me.

"This is new." I greeted him, a little surprised when he kissed my cheek again. "What brought this on?"

He shrugged. "I was getting some for me, and I remembered how you always came in earlier on Mondays. I had a feeling that hadn't changed."

I smiled as I followed him toward the elevators. "Thank you. This is very sweet of you."

We didn't talk on the way up, as there were too many people. Nor did we talk as he walked me to my office. He kissed my cheek quickly and then half ran to his own. I stared at my secretary (how cool was it that I had one now?) who was just as shocked as I was.

"What was that all about?" Linda was a few years older than me and had been with the firm since college.

"I haven't a single clue. He was waiting for me downstairs with coffee when I got here."

She tried to hide her smile by rubbing her lips. I walked into my office, moving this conversation to a more private area. She followed, carrying her tablet.

"Maybe he likes you."

I shook my head and sat in my chair as I put my things away for the day. "No, I don't think so. He came by on Friday to ask me to lunch because he wanted to celebrate the promotion with me. Chris was my boss before this. He is just being nice."

She sat across the desk from me, crossing her legs. "Or he always liked you and thought now that you are equals he can finally do something about it. The celebrating thing could have just been an excuse to get you to go out with him."

"No…" I started to argue, then remembered the odd looks he kept giving me, and how he kept kissing my cheek. "You think?"

She giggled and played with her wedding ring. "My Bruce did that. He made up an excuse about failing a class we had together and begged for my help. I found out later that he was at the top of the class. But by then, I had already been falling in love with him. He confessed it all when I approached him about it, angry that he lied to get me alone." Linda shrugged. "That was the first time he kissed me, to shut me up." She giggled. "I couldn't stay mad at him after that."

Instead of picturing Chris lying to get me alone, I saw Dillan lying to get me up to his studio. I shook it off.

"This could all just be hearsay. I'm not making any judgments until he is open about it, if that is even what this is."

"M'kay." She totally was on that romantic train that happy couples got on.

I sighed and rubbed my forehead. "What's on today's schedule?"

Thankfully, it was a busy one. Mondays always were, which was why I liked getting there early.

My first meeting was with Lawerence, one of the Senior Partners, and a long-time client, Bill White. They had been trying to convince Bill that he needed to upgrade his mobile security. He owned a biotech plant. They needed all the upgrades in my opinion, but this guy had to be spoon-fed. According to the file Linda had given me this morning, that was how they had always handled Bill.

The moment Lawerence looked at me, after many denials from Bill, I knew what he wanted. Apparently someone was gossiping on their floor. My bets were on Kurt. Big mouth.

With a small smile, not upset in the least that they were talking about me in a positive way, I pulled out my phone and hacked into Bill's phone, which was in his front coat pocket. I pulled up all of his social media accounts, and the pictures he had on his phone, then slid it across the table for him to see.

His jaw dropped. "I took that picture just this morning. It hasn't even been uploaded to my cloud yet."

The picture was of his wife feeding who I assumed was their granddaughter in her high chair.

"I hacked your phone, from my cell, within less than 10 minutes. Now will you trust us to upgrade your mobile security? As well as your cloud security?" I reached over and swiped my phone, where all of his pictures on the cloud were. "I stayed out of any of your business folders, but they would be just as easy. The pictures are all I looked at."

He cleared his throat and passed my phone back. "Yes, upgrade it all. Anything you need. I thought we were safe enough."

"Tech progresses every year. We need to make sure your security does as well. It's the only way to keep your business, your family, your whole life, safe." Lawerence stated almost morosely.

The rest of the meeting went smoothly as we explained all the measures that would be taken. When I shook Bill's hand, he leaned in and whispered, "All of the pictures?"

I giggled. "Yes. Don't worry, I quickly swiped past any, uh, personal ones. It's nice to see that you and your wife have such a close relationship, even after all these years. Congratulations. I hope I have that one day."

He blushed and nodded as he quickly walked out.

"Do I want to know?" Lawerence asked in amusement.

I cringed. I hadn't swiped fast enough on the first one and the couple were definitely not in their prime anymore. Nor did he look as good as Dillan had.

"Probably not."

He laughed and collected his things. "I heard the rumors over the years, about your skills with computers. I must say, I was a bit incredulous about it. I'm proud to say I was wrong. And I am even more thrilled that you chose our side. If you had gone the other way, I don't know that we ever would have been able to catch you."

It was my turn to blush as he escorted me out of the room. "Thanks. I love it here. I love helping people feel safe."

"Then you are in the right place, Fiona." He nodded in farewell and then left.

Linda followed me into my office, dying to know what happened. I told her and she laughed. She often said it was nice to see a young woman showing up all the men for a change. The last Junior partner she helped was a bit misogynistic. She had celebrated when he decided to branch out and start his own firm. I had a good laugh when she told me that she frequently threw a dollar coin into the wishing fountain at the mall, wishing for his business to fail and be bought out by a woman.

I didn't see Chris again until after work when he walked me out. Katia was waiting, having been in the area showing a condo to someone. Her eyes lit up when he kissed my cheek goodbye. As soon as he was out of earshot, I pointed a finger at her.

"Don't say it. I've heard enough about it from Linda."

Katia raised her hands up in surrender. "Not gonna say a thing." Once we loaded up and started driving, she changed her mind. "Okay, one thing."

I groaned and closed my eyes.

"He's got that nerdy cute thing going for him. Totally go for it if the door opens."

I whimpered out a pathetic crying laugh. My mind, of course, went to me opening the door as Dillan balanced me in his arms. I really needed to stop thinking about him.

Chris met me every morning with coffee that week and walked me out every evening. It got to the point that I grew used to it and started expecting him at those times. Color me surprised when he showed up in my office again at lunchtime on Friday.

"Can I cash in that rain check now?"

I laughed. "Sure. Why not. Any ideas?" I pulled out my purse and let him escort me to the elevator. Thankfully, Linda had already left for lunch.

We ended up going to a deli nearby. Not a single thing romantic about it. We talked about work mostly, but small things about our outside lives crept in toward the end. For the most part, he kept to his side of the table, giving me distance. Only occasionally touching my hand with his. And when we left, Chris put his hand on my lower back as he held the door for me.

I wanted to feel something for him, but there was nothing there. He was cute. He was smart. He was definitely more my type than Dillan was. If I hadn't met Dillan, I was sure things would have been different with Chris. Hell, when I first started working for him I had a crush on him. Not that I had ever felt that insane attraction with him that I had with Dillan though.

Nothing else could compare.

Chapter 6

Dillan

I wasn't entirely surprised to wake up alone. It wasn't the first time, and usually a preference of mine. I was surprised that I was disappointed that she had left though. When I first started waking up, I entertained the idea of another round. Which obviously wasn't going to happen now.

I stood up and stretched my sore muscles. The kind you got after a good workout. The night before, and half the morning, had proved to be the best kind of workouts. Yawning loudly, I walked toward the small kitchenette, knowing there would be bottles of water in the fridge.

I stopped when I saw the small note and envelope on the table.

With a smile I picked up the note, this was more like Fiona's style. She wouldn't be able to leave without saying goodbye, or not having the last word. That wasn't in her nature. At first I laughed at her comment about the debt, but then confusion took over.

She left a gift?

I spun in a circle around the room but saw nothing out of the ordinary. Maybe I wasn't awake enough to spot it yet. I pulled out a bottle and guzzled it down. I walked over to my dresser to put some pants on at least. There were none there.

Nothing was in that drawer.

"What the hell?" I whispered into the empty room.

I went through every drawer, but they were all the same - as bare as I was. I jogged around the room, looking for my clothes from the night before. But they weren't there either.

I snapped my fingers, remembering that most of my clothes had been removed in the elevator. At least I think they were. My boxers should have still been in the room at least though.

Unless Keith took them as a joke when he left. He would do something like that.

The hall was empty of all clothing items. Shaking my head, I put my finger on the screen and called the elevator. But the light turned red instead of green. I tried again, same response.

Cursing, I went back to the room and searched for my phone. I couldn't find it though. It seemed to be gone too.

I groaned and smacked my head when I remembered it was still in the back pocket of the pants I wore last night. I ran for the far corner where the stairs were, I stopped when my eyes landed on the note and money. I grabbed the money, since I didn't know when I was going to get the elevator working again.

My eyes fell on the note for the third time, and I paused.

"Did she…" I laughed and ran for the stairs, note in hand.

The little minx must have taken my clothes. I half expected to find them sprawled through the stairs. She probably wasn't thrilled about having to take all those stairs down this morning.

Oddly, the stairs were empty as well.

I stopped at the second floor and entered my office. Keith was sitting at the desk, probably getting ready to go over the books from the night before. The computer was still in the waking-up phase.

He laughed when he saw me. "Did you forget something?"

I snorted and headed straight for the small wardrobe I kept with extra clothes. One can never be too safe. "I'm guessing you're not the one who took all the clothes out of the studio." I was pretty sure about that by this point, but…

He shook his head and laughed. "Did your little friend at least have clothes to wear?"

"Probably, she was gone when I woke up." I dropped the envelope and note on the desk before pulling the pants up. "But she left these behind."

He picked up the note and read it. "At least she left the money. What was the gift?"

"I'm thinking it was a set of the Emperor's New Clothes."

Keith laughed. "Possibly. Where do you think she put them?"

"No clue." I pulled the *Indecent* polo over my head. "I am curious to find out. First, though, we need to get that elevator fixed."

He raised an eyebrow at me, as he pulled the money out to count it. "What's wrong with it? It worked fine when I arrived this morning."

"Well, it isn't now. Every time I tried to call it; the light turned red."

Maybe he thought I was nuts or something, because he walked out of the office and over to the elevator. I held my breath, wondering if I was going crazy too. But he was denied access just as I was.

"I'll call Jorge, see if he can figure it out." Keith walked back into the office and over to the safe to put the money away.

But that wouldn't open either. With a grunt, he pulled out his phone. I half listened to him as I logged onto the cameras with the now fully awake laptop.

I couldn't access those either.

"Tell him to get here now. Someone has messed with all of our security." Any amusement I felt a few minutes ago was long gone. I was sliding fast into defense mode.

We both sat anxiously in the office for Jorge to show up, just staring out the one-way mirror that allowed us to watch over the club. There wasn't much to look at right now since we weren't open yet. The day crew was cleaning the place while a couple security guys monitored them. Kent walked in and joined the other bartender with doing inventory. I wasn't expecting him today, but that was fine. Inventory was always a pain.

The only people missing so far were the girls. And most of them would still be asleep. Last call on drinks was nearly an hour before last call on the girls.

Jorge came through the office door not much later, with his own laptop in hand. He was expensive, but one of the best when it came to computers. He was worth the money. He sat down at the desk and got straight to work. Demonstrating exactly why he was worth the money.

"Alright, I had to hack my way in because all of my info was wiped from the system. The good news, no one has tried to access anything at all. It looks like only the users were erased. One fingerprint was added this morning but then deleted a few minutes later. I see a record of it, but no name."

"What did they access?" I asked him in a growl. I had an idea, but it was too unbelievable to accept. Yet, it was also the only thing that made sense.

He clicked a few keys on the keyboard then sighed, defeated. "I'm not sure. The elevator was accessed a few times this morning, and your main computer in here was logged into. All of it was around the same time. Just before noon."

"Which is about when I came up to the office. I went to the studio first, but you were both still asleep, so I went to the club and the basement to do a few things. I came to the office just before noon." Keith explained softly. "I never saw anyone else."

I ran my teeth over my bottom lip and shook my head. "What did the elevator look like when you used it? Were Fiona's clothes still in there?"

Keith thought about it for a minute. "Maybe. I know your stuff was still there. I didn't exactly go through any of it."

I chuckled incredulously and shook my head. He would have noticed if my entire backup wardrobe had been in there.

"You don't think… no way." My friend stared at me with his jaw on the floor.

"I can't think of anyone else who was here. Jorge, fix the elevator, I need to see something."

I waited in silence as Jorge clicked away on the keyboard, his fingers flying in all sorts of directions. I didn't look at him again until he cursed.

"Whoever did this is a freaking genius. I can get in. I can look around. I can access the history. But I can't do anything else. We are, in essence, locked out. Of everything."

I wiped my hand over my mouth and pushed to stand up and walked out. Jorge's fingers went back to flying. Keith followed me silently down the stairs.

As expected, BoBo was outside.

"Hey, boss. Nice to see you can walk straight. Your little friend was a little off balance when she left."

Bingo. Just what I needed. "What time was that at? Tell me everything."

A nervous look came over him as he tried to explain how he offered the ride and she refused. I wouldn't have thought much of her need for privacy considering her opinions on security… and my thoughts stopped there.

I laughed, but it lacked all amusement.

Both men just stared at me warily. "Find me everything you can on Fiona Reynolds." I instructed Keith as I put my hand out.

BoBo handed me the keys to my car. Thankfully, he carried an extra set, in case I lost mine or needed a ride home. Mine were in my pants pocket. Which were most likely sitting in that elevator with all my other clothes.

Jorge was still in the office, looking pale and half-dead when I walked in later that night. I forced him away from the computer, and to eat something before laying him on the couch. He was still asleep when I went home that night. But back at it on Sunday morning.

Sunday night we had a fight scheduled. Things in the club had been interesting, what with our computer systems on complete lock-down. Jorge managed to get approval from the system for us to at least take credit cards in the bar. Keith went out before we opened on Saturday and bought about a dozen lock boxes. I was not thrilled. But we needed to lock cash payments up somehow.

I was starting to regret my decision to not use actual registers in my club.

The poker games weren't too big of a deal, just more low-key than normal. We used a mini card reader, Keith's personal tablet (it was a good thing I trusted him), and a lock box for cash.

The tricky part was going to be the fights. A lot more people were involved. A lot more money. And tension would be running high. BoBo increased security at the fights. Rebecca and Keith were the only ones with the key to the cash boxes - we usually brought in a lot of cash during fight nights.

Needless to say, my nerves were at an all-time high just minutes before the fights were set to start.

I paced the room, not being able to stand still anywhere, wary of something happening. Of someone finding out we were vulnerable at the moment.

As though my fears sprang him to life, Ivan placed himself in front of me.

"Why extra men tonight, Dillan? You expecting trouble?" His eyebrows were creased, and his men stood at attention.

I forced out a small chuckle. "No, but one can never be too safe."

"Your girl not running money like normal. Why everyone tense tonight?"

I held my position firm, not giving off any sign of trouble, only irritation.

"We are not expecting trouble tonight, Ivan. Anything else that may or may not be going on is of no consequence to you. This is my business, not yours. You and your men can stay and bet, enjoy the fights. Or you can head up to the club and enjoy some good music, liquor, and a little company. It's your choice. But stay out of my business or you may not be as free to roam around as you are now."

Ivan frowned, catching my not-so-subtle threat. He wasn't fond of the reminder that he did not control me. The Russians did not have a dog in the fights tonight. He had no need to be here, or in my business. He looked at his men, and around the room again at all of my men.

"We will not be involved with anything tonight. Or for a while. Give you time to clean up mess. When you realize you in over head, come see me." With a nod, he and his goons headed for the back entrance to the club.

My entrance to the club.

They were refused admittance however - much to Ivan's displeasure. Good. He needed to remember who really ran this place. I carefully watched as they left through the actual exit. I was sure they would still find their way into the club.

I made my way over to BoBo. "Message Bunny, tell her to keep Ivan company tonight. He's having a rough night."

BoBo laughed and pulled out his phone. We both knew I would be getting money out of Ivan, one way or the other.

The night went smoothly, thankfully. We had a few close calls, ones that kept us on our toes. But my security detail only had to step up to the men arguing with each other, and they quickly shut their mouths.

Only one man seemed to be paying attention to the lockboxes. BoBo spotted him though and stepped into his line of sight.

The man nearly peed his pants.

I didn't want to push our luck though. So, I canceled any other fights until our little problem was solved.

Monday morning, Keith and I collected all the money from the lockboxes and went to the bank to deposit them. Looking at the way he was holding the canvas bag to his chest, I couldn't help but flash back to Friday night, when Fiona arrived. I chuckled, and he raised a questioning eyebrow at me. I just shook my head.

We walked into the bank, and I wrote my name on a clipboard so I could speak to one of their bankers one-on-one. Then we waited. And waited. Apparently we weren't the only ones who had been waiting for the bank to open again to handle sensitive matters.

After a two hour-long wait, with the bank security eyeing Keith with increasing intensity, we finally got called back.

"Good morning, Mr. Murphy." The man with the nameplate Maxwell Carpenter on his desk shook my hand and waved at a chair, inviting us to sit. "What can I help you gentlemen with this morning?"

"A couple things." I lifted a hand to Keith, who lifted the bag. "We have a fairly large cash deposit to make. Unfortunately, we have had some computer issues over the weekend and had to stick to mostly cash at our club."

"Ee. That must have made for one long weekend."

I nodded with a forced smile. "Yes, it's been very stressful. Thankfully, between personal accounts, and people desperate for a break from reality enough to go to the ATM, we were able to stay open. Now we just need to deposit all this stress and regain access to our business account. Which I am hoping you can also help me with."

He raised his hand for the bag. "Let's see what we can do, starting with getting all that cash put away somewhere safe."

Maxwell opened the bag, his eyes widened, and then he waved a security guard over. He had a bill counter on a shelf near his desk, thankfully. The security guard added another layer of protection as Maxwell ran all the money through the machine.

"Wow. What club do you own?" He asked, sitting back down 15 minutes later, his eyes on all the stacks of money.

"*Indecent*." I relayed to him, proudly.

I swallowed the chuckle when his eyes lit up. He knew of us. He just didn't need to know that money wasn't all from drinks and entrance fees.

We watched and waited as Maxwell filled out the deposit slip for us, whistling at the amount of commas he used. After the slip was signed by both parties, he filled the bag back up with the money and sent it off with the silent protector to take to the back and most likely the vault.

Maxwell then turned to his computer. "Alright, let's see what's going on with your account." He typed in the account number I had written on the deposit slip.

His grimace did not make me feel good.

"Well, I have good news and bad news. Which do you want first?"

I slowly took a breath and tried to reign in the building frustration. What the hell was the problem now?

"Let's start with the good news. Dillan needs a break from bad news for just a moment." Keith answered for me.

Maxwell gulped and nodded; his voice slightly shaky. "The good news is that we can deposit the money without any issue."

My head ticked. I hadn't even thought there would be an issue with that, or I wouldn't have let them take the money to the back yet.

"And the bad news." I pushed through my teeth.

"You are no longer listed as the account holder. You can't make any changes to the way the account is set up."

I shot forward, only to be stopped by Keith's arm across my chest.

"Hold on, take a breath." He whispered to me.

I leaned back into the uncomfortable chair and did as my best friend said. The small makeshift office was silent as I tried to regain my equilibrium. During that time, I mentally ran through the most important details to remember.

I didn't want to cause a scene in a bank.

I doubted the man would lie to a client that was so fruitful to their company.

And this incident went right along with everything else happening at the club.

"Who is listed as the account holder now?" I asked slowly, keeping my jaw, and body, firmly in place.

Maxwell licked his lips nervously as he searched through his records. His hands were shaking, and he was covered in sweat when he turned back to me.

"There is no record of who it is. Every time I try, I get a message saying I don't have clearance for that information. I've heard of messages like this, but never actually seen them before."

"And what does it mean?" I let Keith take over, or that scene I was working to avoid would be coming very soon.

"It means that the owner is someone with very high clearance. Someone with so much pull that only certain people can see their information."

"And…" I practically hissed. I needed a real answer.

"Government officials. High-level government employees. Politicians. Or maybe even the really big stars. People with more money than God, basically."

That was confusing enough to make me pause.

"Has the government frozen the account for some reason?" Thank you, Keith! I hadn't thought of that.

Maybe the siblings had gone to the police after all, and that was why all this was happening. But then… why hadn't the police raided our building yet?

Maxwell shook his head side to side rapidly. His black curls flew around his head. "Oh, no. That would be an entirely different message. I also wouldn't have been able to do the deposit with a freeze."

"Why were we allowed to deposit money into an account that says it does not belong to us?"

Maxwell's eyes jumped from Keith back to me, probably grateful I had let him take over the reins of this meeting. "Well, anyone who has the account number can deposit money into an account. It's really only the withdrawals, changes, and stuff like that that requires the account holder listed."

I startled the man when I randomly pushed out of my seat and stalked out of the office. I headed straight for the exit. Nothing was going to be solved sitting there talking to him.

Keith joined me not two minutes later. I leaned against the building, watching the pedestrians walking by, going about their merry little way. My eyes lifted and scanned all the tall buildings in the city. I couldn't help but wonder if Fiona was in one of those offices right now, looking down on us… laughing at me.

"What now, boss?"

I pushed off the wall, straightened my suit jacket, and looked him dead in the eye. "Now we find us a rat. The only way to fix this is to find the one who did it all."

"And then?"

BoBo pulled up in my black Aviator and stepped out. We chose the bigger car today, so Keith and I could both fit in the back without being squished.

"Then we teach those siblings who the real boss is."

Chapter 7

Dillan

It took three days before we gave up trying to find Fiona. Instead, I went to find Randy. He was much easier to find. Jorge was visibly relieved when he found him within minutes. I was sure Jorge was beginning to doubt his own abilities by that point.

I waited outside Randy's apartment on Thursday night. He got home from work about 9pm. I stepped quietly out from under the staircase that was next to his first-floor apartment. He lived closer to the San Fernando Valley then he did to the downtown LA area, where my club was.

I stayed in the shadows until after Randy pushed his door open and walked inside. I rushed up behind him and shoved him hard enough to make him fly a few feet in and fall on the floor. I had some frustrations to get out. It had not been a good week.

I slammed the door closed behind me and locked it. He rolled onto his butt and crawled away from me. Sticking to the floor. The wrestler in him was probably more comfortable with that. I didn't care. I could work with anything. Besides, he was closer to my boots down there.

"Dillan? What are you doing here? Fi said she gave you everything." He stammered nervously, licking his lips, and looking around the room.

I chuckled darkly and squatted down to his level. "Oh, she did, and then some. Your sister is quite the piece of work."

"Wh... what are you talking about?"

"Where can I find Fiona, Randy? She and I have some unfinished business to discuss."

He gulped and moved further away. "I'm not telling you anything."

I stood back up and did my best to relax my pose. "I mean no harm to her. I just need to have a little chat with her."

Something in Randy clicked into place. His balls, maybe? He stood up, finally not looking like such a weakling.

"What do you want to know? I will tell you what I can, but I won't tell you where she is. Fi likes her privacy."

I snorted and shook my head. "How much does your sister know about computers?"

Randy stepped back, surprised. "What?"

I stepped forward, adding a little menace to my movement and words. "How well… does Fiona… know computers?" I asked slowly and succinctly.

He looked to the side, like he was searching for words. Or how to lie his way out of it.

"Fi knows about as much as anyone, I guess."

"You are such a bad liar. I've watched you play poker for years, Randy. I know all your tells. Now answer the question honestly this time."

He leveled me with a look, his balls coming back out for a brief moment. "Why do you need to know? Why do you care what talents Fiona has?"

I closed the distance between us in two strides, he valiantly tried to keep his firm position. Maybe he wasn't completely hopeless after all.

"I already know about most of your baby sister's *talents*." Randy's eyes widened, catching my meaning. "It's the computer ones I need to know. See, someone messed with all of my computer systems on Saturday morning… around the time she left my apartment above the club…" I chuckled at the look on his face. "She didn't tell you about staying all night, did she? She didn't tell you how she just barely missed the cut-off for your interest, or how I convinced her to pay them off in trade?"

I closed my eyes and rolled my head, smiling. Taunting him was proving to be fun and helping soothe the raging beast a bit.

"Hmmm, your sister has many talents indeed."

I did not expect the fist that hit me right in the nose. I laughed as I wiped it, checking to see if he made me bleed. He didn't.

"Your sister had quite the hit as well when I suggested she stay over. I'm glad to see there are lines for you, Randy. Now. Tell me about your sister and her ability with computers."

The fact that I was unphased by the hit seemed to shake him to the core. His answer came out fast. "Fi works for a computer company. That's all I know. She has always been extremely smart. She received offers from many of the top colleges, with full scholarships, including MIT. But she turned them down to stay local and take care of my Dad and me. That's what she does. She takes care of everyone else. I'm a screwup, we all know that. But not Fi. So please just leave her out of this. She doesn't have a vindictive bone in her body. She would never screw with someone's security on purpose. I'm sure it was all just a coincidence."

I was sure it wasn't. I was willing to bet he only knew the surface level things about his sister. He was good at reading people at the poker table, so why did he suck so bad at reading his own sister?

"How can I find her?" I tried one more time.

He laughed sardonically. "Honestly? You can't. I don't know where she lives. I usually only see her at family dinners with our father. I give her rides home, but I know she is giving me the wrong address. I've seen her get into Ubers after I drop her off. Before today, it bugged me." He waved a hand at me. "Now I think I'm starting to see her point, and her reason for all the paranoia."

I straightened my suit jacket and moved back toward the door. "She's been covering for you since high school, and now is when you realize the danger you put her in?"

His face registered his shock. "She told you about that?"

I shrugged. "I enjoyed talking with your sister. She told me a lot of things." Not things I would share with him, nor were they all that pertinent to the conversation at hand, but I wanted him to think they were.

I walked out and left him to his own thoughts. Part of me worried he would warn her that I was looking for her. But I was fairly certain he wouldn't. Just like I knew there would be no point in following him. Randy was going to do all he could to avoid contact with his sister while I was looking for her.

I stepped into the back of my car, just a basic black town car this time since I wanted to blend into the background, letting BoBo drive. He was very discreet, so he was the best person for the job when I needed it.

I pulled out my phone and called Jorge. "Get me everything you can on Mr. Reynolds. Their father."

His breath released in a relieved sigh. "Oh, that's easy. I already found him. He moved to a nursing home a few months ago. Olympus Prime. Supposed to be one of the best in the state. Expensive too."

I hung up and leaned back in my seat. "I need someone watching the Olympus Prime nursing home this week. If anyone sees Fiona walk in, call me immediately. No one is to approach."

"Yes, sir." BoBo replied, pulling out his own phone.

I listened to his side of the conversation, as he got someone on it.

Work continued to be difficult. I ended up keeping everything, but the club closed all week. Tracking bets without my computer system was a nightmare. Nor did I want to push my luck with all the lock boxes for the cash. This also helped me keep the security focused on just the club and the bar, instead of spreading them out. I really missed my security cameras too. I had plenty of men, but my nerves were wearing on me.

I even had to get a new phone. I still couldn't access anything from my cloud because I was locked out of it as well. It was like starting all over again.

I hated it. I hated starting over.

My anger at Fiona overrode any of the pleasant memories. When I thought about her now, I only saw red.

Sunday afternoon, more than a week after she left my studio and blew up my entire life, I got the call that she was seen at the nursing home. I walked away from Keith and Rebecca mid-sentence. I waved BoBo off when he tried to join me.

For the last few days, I had been driving my one car that did *not* blend in. Mostly because driving fast was my only release these days. If I even tried to get close to a woman, I saw Fiona's brown hair and her sweet seductive smile. I instantly became angry and hard at the same time. No woman wanted to be near me when I was that angry.

Well, okay, there was one, but I refused to touch her. I didn't even like her near me lately since she kept singing Ivan's tune and pestering me that we should just ask him for help. I was beginning to think Bunny had spent far too much time with Ivan.

I lost count of how many times I had to take care of my own personal business, all the while imagining myself strangling the life out of that little siren. Her voice and beauty had called to me, and the second I was under her control, she nearly destroyed me.

An hour later, thanks to LA traffic, I pulled into the back of the parking lot at the nursing home. With a wave, I dismissed the man watching the place, and took up his post.

Five very long hours of stewing only added to my frustrations. Randy had arrived a couple of hours after me. Which meant this was most likely when they met for their family dinners. I wasn't surprised that she spent more time here than he did.

Around seven, I saw both of them coming out, walking in the direction of his car. I stepped out of mine and approached them from behind.

"Think I will give the princess a ride home tonight, Randy."

Randy jumped and dropped his keys. Fiona just sighed with acceptance but kept her back to me.

"Uh. no. It's alright. I can take her." Randy stumbled through, trying to find his keys.

"Go home, Randy. I got this. Dillan isn't going to hurt me." The sound of her calm voice both angered and turned me on. Which just ticked me off more.

Fiona finally spun around to face me, and all of my ire bled out. How the hell had I forgotten about her pull on me?

"Are you, Dillan?"

I blinked, realizing she was still talking. My bad. "No." I croaked embarrassingly, then cleared my throat. "No. We just need to talk."

She gave me a half smile and moved over to pick up the keys for her dimwitted brother, who was too busy watching us to find his own keys by his feet. My eyes moved to that perfectly rounded butt when she bent over. I smirked when Randy glared at me. He caught me checking out his little sister, and I didn't care.

"Go home, Randy. I'll call you tomorrow." She leaned over and kissed his cheek. "Drive safe. And go straight home. Please."

Her plea to him about broke me.

Randy sighed and nodded but did not agree to anything. Something she did not miss. As soon as he was gone, I pulled out my temporary phone with one hand, putting it to my ear, and placed my other on her lower back, directing her to my car. I didn't miss the small shiver she gave when I touched her. It made me smile.

Good to know the pull still went both ways.

"You good? Do I need to send a clean-up crew?" He picked up on the first ring, as I knew he would.

I huffed. "No. Just let me know if Randy shows up."

"Got it, boss." Keith hung up and I put my phone away.

"Thank you." Fiona mumbled as we walked.

I nodded in response and unlocked my car.

I opened the back door of my dark blue Porsche SUV for her, and she slid in. I stepped in after her, then locked the car again before setting both my phone and key fob in the cup holder.

"Um, what are we doing back here?" Fiona looked around the car and out the window, no doubt nervous.

"Like I said, we need to talk."

She hummed quietly, her eyes landing on my stupid phone, then cracked a grin. "Get a new phone?"

The last string of my sanity snapped. I grabbed her face and roughly turned her to me, just before slamming my lips onto hers. She matched me for intensity, just like I knew she would. I frantically worked at her pants, while she worked at mine. We both paused when our bodies were reunited, moaning out in satisfaction.

It was a very short pause.

She stayed on my lap, completely naked, as our bodies cooled back down. I held her tight to me, her head tucked in my neck.

"Thought you wanted to talk." She mumbled, tiredly.

I huffed and rubbed my hand up and down her back. "That was the plan. This wasn't. I can't seem to keep my hands off you when you are around."

She yawned and burrowed into my neck, kissing it softly. "Same." She tried to sit up, but I only let her go so far.

"You screwed with my system. With my entire business."

To her credit, she didn't deny it. "You lied about the interest."

I cringed. "How did you know?"

"I'm a light sleeper. I heard you and your man talking about it."

This time I hmm'd and kissed her softly. "And yet you stayed."

Her arms wrapped around my neck again. "I wasn't sure if it was a dream or not. Someone didn't really give me time to think much about it when I was fully awake."

"I didn't hear any complaining."

She giggled and pulled the hair on the back of my head, giving her access to my neck. I swiftly rotated us, so her back was on the seat, and I was hovering over her. My expensive cars were always worth the extra space and power.

I lifted her leg and spanked her. Fiona's eyes rolled to the back of her head.

"You locked me out of my whole system. Even my computer guy couldn't gain access. I think he is half in love with you just from that. If he ever sees you, he will worship you."

"Why is…" she moaned loudly, making me grin as I moved within her, "that?"

I stopped moving, making her frown. "Because you are the most beautiful thing I have ever seen. I was ready to kill you all week. I've been waiting out here for hours, planning how to torture answers out of you, and then how to kill you without anyone knowing. But then I took one look in your hypnotizing eyes, heard one word in your siren voice, and all the anger fled from me. What is this power you have over me?"

Fiona didn't respond, she just thrust her hips up, forcing me to refocus on the task at hand. Literally. As one hand was on her chest, while the other kept me from falling on top of her.

I waited until we were both dressed again before speaking. "Seriously, I need access to my computers and accounts. We can't even open the safe to put the money in every night. I've had to hire extra security, so the clients don't try anything on my employees to get that money."

With a smirk, she pulled out her phone and looked like she was messaging someone.

"Done." She slid her phone back in her purse not even five minutes later.

"That's it? It's all open now?"

"Yep. And I ordered an Uber, they should be here soon."

Well, now I was offended. "I said I would take you home. I know you told BoBo no because you didn't want me to find you. And I know you don't tell Randy because who knows who all is following him trying to collect money. But I already found you. And I don't care about him."

Fiona laid her head on my shoulder, much in the way Bunny does sometimes, with her hand on my chest. Unlike Bunny though, I didn't want Fiona to move away. I needed to keep her there longer. But why?

"It's not just you and Randy. There is only one person out there who knows where I live and where I work. It's more because of my job than anything else." She rotated her head enough to look up at me, I responded by tightening my hold on her. "It's kind of my job to both protect people from hackers and to catch the hackers when they try."

"Ah, hence you hiding your cyber footprint." That explained a lot.

Fiona giggled again and hugged my waist. "Just how hard did you try to find me?"

I tipped her chin up with my finger, kissing her softly. "Jorge has barely slept all a week, my computer guy. I've had people scouring the city for you. I visited your brother the other day, but he was a bit harder to crack than I expected. Guess he does have a protective streak for you. Jorge did find your Dad, so someone has been out here watching. The minute you showed up today, they called me. I've been waiting out here for you to come out."

She practically purred as I held her. "All that because I locked you out? What would you have done if I crashed your system and took all of your money?"

I growled at her playfully, holding her tight enough to make her squeak. "Try me, princess."

She started laughing but stopped when a car pulled into the parking lot. "That would be my ride."

"No, you are in your ride. I am taking you home. And you will tell me truthfully where you live."

Fiona tried to move away but I wouldn't let her. She was stuck.

"Dillan."

"Fiona."

She glared at me. "No. You do know what that word means don't you?"

I had an idea on how to keep her, which she discovered when she saw my wicked grin.

"No, no more deals."

I roughly moved her to my lap, causing her to squeal again. "You will want to hear this one. Let me take you home tonight, let me stay with you…" her eyebrows went up with that last part, which made me want to laugh, "and I will make sure Randy no longer gambles in my games." I frowned slightly. "I can promise he won't gain access to my place, but I can't promise for the others. I will try, but there is no guarantee."

"You would do all that, for just one night with me?"

"Yes, princess." I was pretty sure I would do almost anything for one more night with her. Not that I was going to tell her that.

I pulled her down for another kiss and her phone dinged. She let me pick it up, and watched as I canceled her Uber. She lost her clothes again after that.

Fiona lived in an apartment downtown, with a doorman and security in the lobby. I would have to see about bribing them to keep me informed. I worried about both her job and her brother's mistakes to the wrong people.

Her apartment was much nicer than Randy's. I had a feeling the main reason he never saw it was because she didn't want him to think she had more money than she did. Well, how much she *used* to have. Before she paid me and who knew how many other people because of him.

I wasn't offered a tour, nor did I ask for one. She closed the door, set down her purse, and walked out of the living room. I only knew it was okay for me to follow because she dropped her clothes on the floor along the way. I dropped mine right on top of them.

I stood in the doorway, wearing nothing but my boxers, as I watched her take off the last two items of material. I could have offered to help, but I was too busy enjoying the show. The black cotton underwear, which were most likely destroyed after our time in the back seat of my car, and her basic white bra, hit the floor as she turned around to face me.

I slowly took in every inch of her body with my eyes, engraving it to memory.

She sat on the edge of the bed, leaning back onto her elbows, and took her turn to watch me. I slowly pushed my last bit of clothing off and onto her hardwood floors. I stalked closer to her, rubbing up and down the one thing she couldn't take her eyes off of. As I got closer, she scooted back enough to be completely on her Queen size bed. I slid in as I lowered onto her perfect body.

We only left the bed long enough to eat a snack, she insisted it be actual food and not just her. I wasn't convinced, but I let her heat up leftover chicken and potatoes for us. Apparently, she liked to cook. And she was good at it.

While we were taking that needed break to refill our strength, we talked about people in our lives. She told me about her friend Katia, who helped her get a great deal on the condo she now owned.

I told her about how Keith and I met. We were both freshmen in college and were struggling. We both worked doing odd jobs, until I had the bright idea to start a poker tournament. Keith was the muscle. I was the money man. I completed my bachelors in business. He completed one in accounting. Now he was the money man. Our business built up from there.

I told her about us living in that small studio apartment together when we first bought the building, having depleted our funds even with the loan from the bank.

"Curious question." She turned to face me from where she sat on my lap while we talked and ate.

I told her it was the only way I'd let her out of bed. It was her idea for us to share the plate, and the glass of wine. She said it was to save dishes.

"What's that?" I opened my mouth as she fed me another bite of potatoes.

"When Keith came in the other night, was he still there when you woke me up?"

I nearly choked on my food. I hadn't thought about that part when she mentioned overhearing us talking. She took that as my answer and smacked my bare shoulder.

"I can't believe you!"

I swallowed then took a quick drink before talking. "I wasn't really thinking about him. I was only thinking about getting back inside of you. The moment I lifted the blanket off you, I forgot about him completely. Right up until I heard the door close."

She groaned and curled under my neck, as though she were trying to hide from the truth.

"He saw more of me than he did of you." I tried consoling her. It felt uncomfortable in my chest when she was upset.

"Why would he stay and watch you like that? Is he gay or something?"

I laughed and turned her all the way around to face me. I explained the setup from when he and I had lived together, she laughed.

"That's gross. I love Katia, she is my best friend. But I don't ever want to see her naked or getting it on with Andy. It's bad enough knowing when they are doing it in another room."

I chuckled as I kissed her cheek. "It's not like we are watching each other, it's more the act itself. Haven't you ever watched porn?"

"Ew, no."

I couldn't help but kiss her after that. "Maybe it's different for guys. We were too broke for porn. And there was always one of us that was too busy to find someone. It was a stressful time, and the release was needed."

"You don't still…"

"Hell, no." I cut her off. "We have our own places. The other day was the first time in years. And I had just been talking about this incredible pull you have on me. Just talking about you made me so hard my boxers failed to hide me. He was probably just curious. And, as I said, I forgot he was in the room."

She curled into me again with a yawn. "I get it. The world just disappears for me when you are around, too."

From the sound she made next, I was pretty sure she fell asleep. Someone really needed to be here to make sure she was taken care of the way she takes care of everyone else.

I carried her back to the bed before going and taking care of our plate and downing the last of our wine. She had already cleaned everything else up.

With that done, and double checking the locks on the door, since we had been a bit distracted when we came through earlier, I joined the intoxicating woman in the bed. I barely had my arms around her when Fiona curled into me again.

I fell asleep with a smile on my face.

Chapter 8

Fiona

The first thing I saw when my eyes opened was the bare chest in front of me. The first thing I felt was something much lower than that, and in perfect position seeing as I had one leg over both of his. Feeling playful, and knowing I probably still had a few minutes before my alarm would go off - I really only set it as a backup in case I overslept, something I'd never done (I didn't count the night I spent with him before, I had hardly slept that night) - I slid one hand around to his back and rocked my hips forward. Dillan was still asleep, but his body reacted, trying to reach me. I repeated my movement, making it try harder to get to me.

That was all it took. I was on my back a second later, getting impaled. Just as I wanted.

It wasn't until his sweaty chest was pressed against mine, both our breathing rapid, that I registered the alarm clock beeping in the background.

I pouted. "I have to go to work."

Dillan kissed my shoulder and pushed up enough for me to see him better. "Call in sick. Tell them you are bedbound today. I'll make it so you aren't lying."

I laughed, then laughed again when his eyes rolled to the back of his head. I didn't get up for a few more minutes.

He tried to follow me to the shower. I firmly said no and then locked him out of the bathroom. By the time I got out, I could smell bacon and eggs frying. I dressed quickly, then joined him.

"Hope you don't mind, I helped myself to your fridge." He handed me a glass of orange juice and I took a sip. "Are you hungry?" He lifted the pan of eggs and carried it to the table.

"Starving." I answered, as I followed him to where one plate with bacon sat.

He poured all the eggs onto the same plate. I grinned and waited, curious if he was going to do what I suspected.

Sure enough, after putting the pan back on the stove, Dillan sat down before pulling me onto his lap. Just like the night before. Only this time, he fed both of us. It took a little longer, but it was so much better.

"Let me take you to work." Dillan begged against my lips, again, as he kissed me goodbye at the front door.

"No. I can't. No one can see you."

He frowned and stepped back. "Why?"

Oh joy, I insulted him. I quickly grabbed his shirt and pulled him back. "My bosses can't know I have ties to the underworld. No matter how small they are."

Dillan still wasn't happy about that, but he let it go. "When will I see you again?"

I bit my lip to keep from smiling. "Do you want to see me again? I thought it was just one night. A deal."

He brushed his fingers through my hair, something I knew he liked to do. Which was why my hair was almost always going to be down now. Just in case. Yeah, I was pathetic, I know.

"I think we both know that deal was just my way of giving you something you wanted."

"Hmmm, and here I thought it was your way to weasel your way into seeing me naked again. Something *you* wanted."

He chuckled softly as he kissed my forehead. "Do I need to keep creating reasons to see you naked? Or is my desire to be with you going to be enough now?" He took my hand and placed it over said desire.

I whimpered, because now I was the one with a need. I unzipped his pants and slid my hand in. I grinned when he hissed.

"Is that what this is? Desire? And here I thought you were just horny."

Dillan's head fell back, his eyes closed. "It is most definitely that too. But only for you."

"Really? No one else is going to touch you? Not even your little friend from the club?" I may have squeezed a little too tight when I thought of her draped all over him.

Dillan jumped but didn't move away. Instead, he made a mess all over himself. He cursed and sank against the wall. I removed my hand and wiped it on his shirt.

Dillan grabbed my hand and pulled me in close. "Bunny is nothing but an employee. I've never touched her, or anyone that works for me. I swear to you."

"That's not what it looked like."

"It was supposed to look like that. She is one of the few open for private rooms. When she needs to tell me something, she acts like she is coming onto me. It helps hide her purpose and sell herself to customers."

I shook my head, looking away from him. "She wants you."

Dillan cringed. "Yes. But she knows the answer already." He put a finger to my cheek and turned me back to face him. "You are the one I want. No one else. I can promise you that."

"I don't want her even pretending."

He shrugged. "Done. No more. The only woman to touch me from now on, real or fake, will be you. Better?"

I bit my lip, trying not to smile and squeal like a lovesick teen, and nodded. "Yes." My phone dinged, letting me know the Uber was waiting. "I have to go to work. I'm later than normal for a Monday. Stay for as long as you need to, in order to clean up the mess you just made." I waved a finger up and down his front, pointing out his dirty clothes.

He chuckled and kissed me one more time before opening the door.

I grinned all the way to work, reliving that last talk over and over again.

I grinned all the way up until I walked through the lobby doors.

Where the grin promptly slipped off my face. "Chris." Oops.

"Hey, are you okay? You're running a little late today." He handed me the coffee. "It's a bit cold now."

"It's fine. Thank you. And yeah, I'm fine, just had a long night and overslept."

He called the elevator then stepped back to stand with me. "You aren't getting sick, are you? We don't want you to overdo it."

"I'm fine, really. Just have a lot going on right now." We stepped into the blessedly full elevator, with those who had boarded up in the underground parking lot. Full elevators meant no more third-degree.

This time when he kissed me at my office, I flinched away. Less than an hour ago I was telling Dillan no woman could touch him if we were going to make a go of this, and here I had another guy kissing me. Chris frowned slightly at my flinch as he walked away. I felt bad. I went to lunch with him last week, where I gave signals that I might be open to trying something. Hell, I even let him hold my hand during lunch.

Now here I was, flinching!

Linda followed me to my office, closing the door behind her. She studied me as I moved around my office, preparing for the day.

She cursed softly. "You slept with someone and it sure as hell wasn't Chris."

"Say what now?" I asked stupidly, sitting down. My thighs were sore.

She sank into her usual chair and grinned. "You slept with someone."

"Huh, what? No."

She laughed happily. "Girl, you are moving like someone nearly broke you last night. And I really don't think Chris has the power to do that. Not to mention how you moved away from him out there."

I cringed. "Was it that obvious?"

She waved it away. "Not really. I was watching. Obviously Chris noticed when you moved away, but that's it."

I sank deeper into my chair. "What do I do?"

She leaned forward eagerly. "You mean there is someone? Why didn't you say something before?"

"Because I didn't know it was possible. He's an acquaintance of my brother. We spent time together a couple of weeks ago, and I didn't think I'd see him again. I ran into him yesterday; he's been looking for me. Mostly because I hacked into the security system of his company and locked him out, but he deserved it. One thing led to another, and another, and… well, you get the point. He was still at my place when I left this morning." I nibbled on the nail of my thumb as I looked at her nervously. "He says he wants to make a go of this. He even agreed to not touch any other women, or they him. And then I get here, and Chris is here, acting normal…" I dropped my head on my desk.

"Oh, sweetie, it's okay." Why did it sound like she was laughing at me?

"What do I do, Linda?" I sat up and looked at her. "I don't want this to interfere with work."

She put on her business-as-usual face and sat up, her tablet in her lap. "First off, you never agreed to anything with Chris, you were friendly, that was it. That should be easy to take care of. Plus, you no longer work under him. This should not affect your work."

"How is it easily taken care of though?" Yeah, I begged.

Linda waved it away and woke up her tablet. "Just have the new boyfriend show up to take you to lunch, or bring you to work, anything like that. It will settle the matter without any confrontation. Chris isn't the kind for that anyway. It will be a blow to his ego…" She trailed off and paused as she looked at me for confirmation.

"Oh, yeah. Dillan is far from a nerd. Think… Greek God."

"Definitely an ego blow then. But that's it."

"There might be one slight problem. I told Dillan not to come around. I am trusting you to keep your mouth shut with this…" I waited while she zipped her lips. "Dillan may or may not have a few hands in a few underground businesses." I grimaced, waiting for the fallout and for her to tell me how stupid I was being.

She didn't.

"Yeah, so. All that really matters is if he cares about you, honors you, and treats you like a queen. Does he?"

I sighed. "He does. The night we met he carried me because my feet were sore."

"See, then there you go."

"But the Senior Partners…"

Linda put the end of her stylus in her teeth as she mentally debated that one. "I see what you mean there. Maybe he is better staying away, for everyone's sake." She tapped her tablet a few times as she spoke. "We will think of something, don't worry. Now, you have a meeting with your team in about ten minutes. Pull it together."

I deflated as soon as she left. I should have stayed in bed with Dillan.

We hadn't exchanged numbers yet. Not that it really mattered for me. It only took about two minutes before I had his new number. Unfortunately, it was time for my meeting. At least they would be coming up to me in one of the conference rooms. I really needed to keep the walking to a minimum today.

Chapter 9

Dillan

I couldn't help but smile as I went to Fiona's bathroom and found a washcloth. That woman practically ripped my manhood off when she thought of Bunny touching me. I was fairly certain it was more her jealousy and not the pain that got to me. I loved it.

Fiona was an enigma through and through. She was the perfect example of a sinner hiding as a saint. She loved her job. I had no doubts about that. I was also pretty sure her bosses wouldn't care about me. As far as most of the world was concerned, I was just a club owner. But I could see her point. And I would respect her wishes. No matter how much I hated them.

I cleaned myself off as well as I could, then headed to the lobby. The same doorman and security were on duty again. I approached the security guard and talked to him softly.

"I don't know if you remember…"

"You came in with Fi last night."

I tipped my head to the side and nodded, impressed.

"You have a good memory."

He shrugged. "Fiona needs looking after. She is too nice for her own good."

I couldn't help the small chuckle. "I agree, but only to a degree. Fiona is most definitely capable of handling herself. She just puts her own needs last."

He frowned but nodded.

"I will be around for a long while." I pulled one of my business cards out of my wallet, with a hundred folded behind it. "I would appreciate a heads-up if anything happens. Her brother does not associate with the best of people, and I worry about it falling back on her."

"And how do I know you are telling the truth? How do I know she wants you around?" He didn't move to take the card or money.

I lifted an eyebrow and waved the small items back and forth. "Fiona bring men home often? She really seem like the type to let people she doesn't trust know where she lives? Or even stay after she leaves?"

He thought about that then nodded as he emptied my hand. "That is true. Very true. I have her brother on a list of no admittance. In fact, she strictly said to tell him she does not live here, and I don't know her, if he tries." He waited expectantly, but I wasn't going to fill in any blanks for him. He sighed when he realized that. "Just please tell me if he is a danger to her. I like Fi. And not just for the cookies or free IT help."

"IT help? Don't you guys have your own?"

"Yeah, but Fi is better." He leaned down like he was telling an earth-shattering secret. "Don't tell anyone, but Fi upgraded all of our systems, and made it so it looked just like the old one. I'm the only one who knows."

I laughed and scratched my head. That woman.

"Yeah, she locked me out of my own company. My computer guy was able to look in, like window shopping. But that was it. Anything connected to electronics was unavailable to us. It was not easy finding her, but totally worth it."

The guard laughed, as did I. 24 hours ago, I was angry enough to kill her over it. Now? It made me want to take her all over again. The surface and place didn't matter, as long as I could be with her.

Living with Keith, and running a nightclub, had nullified my concerns about audiences. In fact, it was after one of the times he had a girl over that I decided to install the cages for the dancers.

Keith had met a girl while scouting other clubs and brought her home. She was just drunk enough that she didn't mind me watching as she danced for him. Or maybe just drunk enough that she hadn't noticed that I was still awake when she first started.

Keith and I both watched, from our perspective beds, as she slowly took one item off at a time. When she was down to her matching leopard skin underwear, Keith tried to join. She slapped him away, laughing. She did a whole number, teasing him, showing him bits and pieces, but all the while kept her distance from him. By the time she was sliding onto his lap, I was reaching for tissues to clean up the mess on my bed.

By that point, Keith and I had been living together for a year. We didn't care about a lot of things anymore. Especially after that. The first time I brought a girl home, he wasn't there. So, we weren't being careful. I was sitting on the couch with my back to the door, and she was on my lap, going for a ride. I didn't know he was there until she paused for a split second. He walked around to the side and sat on the couch, his eyes on her chest while she bounced.

It was a little disconcerting when he opened his pants and started rubbing, within my line of sight. Her intensity though, took my mind off it. The way she shoved my head down to her chest helped too.

A week later, I walked in on him, almost in the same position. He was lying on his back. He never paused and neither did she. As I watched the girl on his lap, I understood his attraction to watching the deed. I paused though when she crooked a finger at me.

Curious, I stepped over. She immediately bent down and took up where my hand had left off. She didn't miss a beat with either of us.

She was the first, but not the last woman that we shared. Most of the time, we took turns. I remember coming out of the bathroom once to see Keith sinking into the girl I had brought home. I laughed.

Another night, his date came into my bed by accident. I took advantage of it. She was embarrassed at first when I flipped her onto her back and pushed my way in. Her face showed a little guilt when Keith looked down at her from over my shoulder. I knew what he wanted, so I rotated us, letting her have the top again. He stepped right up, pulled her chin down - the poor girl was so confused she let him - then pushed his own way into her. It took her a moment to get into it, but one good smack on the butt was all she needed.

My princess loved a good smack on the butt too. I never planned on sharing her with Keith though. I didn't plan on sharing her with anyone - not that she would let me even if I tried. I wanted all her attention and energy focused on me, and only me.

I shook myself out of my thoughts as I tried to remember what we were talking about.

"To answer your question, no, her brother will not harm her. He loves his sister; he's just got his own problems that may backsplash onto her one day." Ones that wouldn't involve me.

Ones that she wouldn't be able to pay off for him.

"Thank you. That is helpful. Fi had said he was no danger, but her actions say otherwise." The security guard lifted the card into the air, the money already in his pocket.

I nodded once and left the building. If the doorman was of any use, I was sure the guard would let him know.

I swung by my place to shower and dress before going to the club. I needed to check in on things, seeing as I left in the middle of the planning meeting for this month's extracurricular activities, and never returned. No one had called me, so I figured that meant things ran smoothly.

I arrived at the club a couple of hours later. BoBo took my seat and parked the car for me. I didn't trust anyone else with my cars. Not even Keith.

Keith was doing a quick inventory at the bar with Kent, preparing for the Monday night rush. You would think we wouldn't be as busy during the week, but people hated Mondays and generally needed to forget they happened.

I patted my best friend's shoulder and signaled for him to follow me. I made my way to the elevator and froze with my thumb in the air. I had access to the accounts this morning, so this should work as well. Growing a pair, I placed my thumb on the pad.

The light turned green, and we both cheered.

Keith chuckled out a curse from behind me, relieved. "About time. How did you get her to fi…x…"

The elevator doors opened, and our jaws dropped.

"Guess we found your clothes." He laughed so hard that Kent came running over. BoBo too. Then they joined in the laughter.

I searched the pile for my phone, then did my own colorful cheer again.

"How did you get it open? Did the little skunk really do all this?" BoBo was still a little bitter that she kept getting the better of him.

I couldn't blame him. It was hard to take her seriously with how innocent she looked.

"Yes, Fiona was behind all of this. And from now on, if she shows up, you call me immediately."

"Don't worry, no one will let her in." BoBo nearly snarled.

I laughed and kicked my clothes to the side so I could stand on the floor of the elevator. "No, you misunderstand. She's mine now. You will make sure she is safe at all times. We will allow her to keep living in private, we will not let word get out about our relationship. It could affect her job, that is why she is so secretive."

The three morons stared at me like they didn't understand anything I just said.

"Fiona Reynolds is now my girlfriend. If she comes by, I want to know. If she is harmed, I expect you to protect her. She is part of our family now, and we take care of our own. But we will also keep her safe by not letting on that she is tied to us. Understand?"

They all nodded mutely.

"And Randy?" Keith asked, still a bit dumbfounded.

"Is no longer allowed to play our tables. He should be banned from all tables in the city if we can manage it." I winked. "I had to promise something to get her to let me in last night. After that, it was easy to convince her to be mine."

Now they laughed. This part of me they were familiar with.

Keith kicked more clothes over and stood next to me as we ascended toward the office.

"This is a change. I thought you were going to kill her."

"Honestly, I planned many ways to do just that. She knows it too. But the minute her eyes met mine, all the fight bled out of me." I shook my head. "I don't get it, but I'm done fighting it."

Keith squeezed my shoulder. "I'm happy for you. You look happy."

"I am happy. Oh, and she was awake that night when you were in there. She said no more spying." I shrugged and walked out. "Sorry."

He grumbled sarcastically. "You saying I need to find my own entertainment?"

"Yep, you can't have mine."

He followed me into the office like a loyal puppy. "You two still forget about the world when you are together?"

I laughed as I opened my laptop, knowing where he was going with this. "You are going to get me in trouble, and I just got her. "

He shrugged, not really caring.

I sat down at my desk, preparing to catch up on a lot of work we hadn't been able to do. My new (soon to be spare) phone dinged with a message. I didn't recognize the number, but something told me that was okay.

Unknown: I should have taken you up on your offer.

I laughed.

Me: And what offer was that?
Unknown: To stay in bed.

"Who is it?" Keith tried looking over my shoulder at my phone. "An unknown number?"

"Yes, we didn't exactly get around to swapping numbers. We were busy sorting out other things. My girl is too smart though." I quickly updated the name and saved her number.

Me: It's not too late. Run to the bathroom, pretend to throw up, and I will be there in a few minutes to pick you up. What street is your building on again?
MyPrincess: har, har, har, Nice try.
Me: What's wrong?

Keith tapped my shoulder a few times, and I absentmindedly moved out of the chair so he could take it.

MyPrincess: I hate Mondays.

The laugh just came out of me like a bomb exploding, making Keith jump. He jumped even higher when Jorge burst through the door.

"I got a notification from the system alerting me to a new sign-in. I didn't get that when she first hacked in. But I just used the elevator, Kent said I could. What happened? How did you get back in?" He huffed and puffed like he had run up the stairs instead of standing in an elevator.

"The boss wooed the hacker and has a new girlfriend." Keith explained nonchalantly, turning the computer around to show him the accounting page. "See, all access. We're back in."

Me: What happened? You were fine when you left.
MyPrincess: I forgot about a certain friend at work. I hadn't exactly been giving signals for either way. He is very nice, and I don't want to hurt him.

I frowned. I didn't like the sound of that.

Me: Please let me show up. Let me handle it.
MyPrincess: My secretary said the same thing. She thought it would be easier. Until I hinted about what you do. She agrees now that keeping you away from the partners is for the best.

I cursed. Both of the other heads in the room turned to me.

"There is a coworker that likes Fi, but she wants to handle it with kid gloves. She won't let me make an appearance."

"Why?" Jorge sat on the desk, facing me.

He would be a good sounding board for this. He made too much money off me to be a risk. And he knew I would kill him, or one of the others would do it for me.

"She said something about it being her job to protect people from hackers and to find the hackers when they try. What kind of job is that? Why would her bosses not want her to associate with me?"

Jorge at least looked like he understood. "Cybersecurity. Basically, you bagged yourself a cyber cop."

I frowned. "She's not a cop though." I looked at my feet. "At least I didn't think so."

"Well, no. Probably not. But just like there are private military companies, there are also private cyber security companies. They run like any other company. They have clients they serve, just like private security. With her hacking skills, she is probably successful at what she does."

"Yeah, she said that's why we couldn't find her. She is wary of other hackers and such."

Jorge nodded, more relaxed then I'd seen him in over a week. "I'm sure any number of criminals would love to get their hands on someone as talented as her. She would be prime picking. You're a good choice for her. If she was willing to go public, no one would dare to touch her. The bad guys don't mess with you."

"Her job isn't the only thing that will get her into trouble." Jorge turned to Keith curiously. "Her brother was a regular at the poker tables. You remember the amateur we threw into that fight a couple weeks ago?"

Jorge's eyes widened when he caught on, then turned back to me.

"She came in to pay off the rest of his debt." I leaned back on the couch, a proud grin on my face. "I conned her into staying the night."

Jorge laughed. "Let me guess, she found out the truth and got her revenge."

"Yeah, pretty much. You think there is any chance she will let me come out of hiding?"

"Nope." Jorge stood up and picked up his laptop bag. "More than likely, it's in her contract not to associate with criminals and such like that. Her brother is a big enough issue. I doubt anyone there knows about him either. Since all is well, I am going to go home and get drunk while beating the tar out of a bunch of teenagers online. See ya later."

He waved as he left.

"I've never been someone's dirty little secret before, might be kind of fun."

Keith laughed at me and went back to inputting all the accounting info from during our lockout time.

Me: I will respect your decision. For now. But if he tries anything…

MyPrincess: You will be the first to know. Thank you. What changed your mind?
Me: I talked to my computer guy. He made some guesses about your job… any chance you have handcuffs…
MyPrincess: No. But I'm sure you can handle that. Must I do everything?

Kent came in then, carrying the inventory sheet, so we could finally make a real order. More than once recently, we had to hit up the various liquor stores and buy stock with cash. Our usual distributor was not happy when he found out. It wasn't our fault we couldn't get a hold of him over the phone. Or even find his number… since that was saved onto my cloud.

We got busy with work, but never too busy that I couldn't occasionally send my girl a message.

As soon as she got off work, Fiona messaged me. I was sitting on her couch when she walked in.

"How did you get in here?" She set her purse on the little table, then made her way to me.

I waited there for her, then pulled her on my lap. "You aren't the only one with skills. Mine are just in the physical realm."

My hand was already inside her shirt, so she barely hummed as she kissed me. "Care to demonstrate?"

"Gladly."

Seconds later, she was on her bare back on the cool hardwood floors. We heated them up quickly.

"I missed you today." I admitted as I kissed her shoulder a few minutes later.

She leaned up enough to lick a bit of sweat off my chest. "I missed you too. Messaging you throughout the day made it easier."

"And the co-worker?" It had been bugging me all day.

"Is just a friend, always has been. It wasn't until recently that he started showing interest. I didn't even know what he was doing. My secretary had to clue me in. I will find a way to let him down gently. I don't want to hurt him or cause problems at work."

"Don't wait too long to talk to him. The longer it is, the more time he has to get his hopes up."

Fiona sighed and laid her head back on the floor. "I know. It might already be. I let him take me to lunch on Friday. He said he wanted to celebrate my promotion, but we hadn't had the chance. He had asked the week before, but I was headed for the bank to get that money. I asked for a raincheck, which he cashed in on Friday."

"Speaking of money..." I regretfully left her on that floor, the sight of her laying there, her body available for my viewing pleasure, made it worth it though. I walked over to the counter and picked up the envelope. "I do believe this belongs to you."

Fiona stood up and walked over to me, taking the envelope gingerly. "But... this was to pay off Randy's debt."

"I don't care about Randy or his debt. I care about you and your safety."

"I am safe." She argued.

"You have sacrificed too much for too long, Fi."

"But that's my job. To take care of them."

"Well, now it's my job to take care of you. Use this money to buy a car. I'd buy it for you, but…"

"I won't let you." She finished for me. "That's what this money was for."

I nodded. "I kind of figured. I also put in the 5 you gave him the week before."

Fiona pushed the envelope into my chest. "I can't. It wouldn't be right."

I took it from her hand and set it on the counter, then wrapped her in my arms. "It wouldn't be right for me to keep your money. Randy's debt has been paid, that is what the books show. This is me taking care of my girlfriend, the only way she will let me. I would have just had Jorge transfer the funds into your account, but I wasn't sure you would appreciate the cyber trail. Why are you crying?" I freaked a little there at the end as I started wiping tears off her face.

Instead of answering, she just kissed me. I was good with that.

Chapter 10

Fiona

The rest of the week passed in a blur. I lived in a nearly constant state of bliss. I woke up every morning to a man I had never dreamed I would have. Then I went to the job I'd dreamed of having for years. And ended my days wrapped in the arms of the same dream man. Some nights he came over later if there were fights or tables being run. His business was up and running like normal again. When Dillan snuck into my apartment late at night, he would slide right into me and the bed.

It was times like those that made me grateful I had gone for the IUD option. Dillan and I did eventually have that talk. I was surprised when he said it had been over two months since he last slept with someone, before me. As for me, it had been nearly a year. We were both clean, and there were no risks. He insisted we celebrate. On the kitchen table. And then he happily bought me a new one.

I half expected Chris to invite me to lunch again on Friday, but he seemed to be getting the point. I hadn't reciprocated the cheek kiss all week, so he was beginning to step back.

Friday night, I got a message from Dillan that said he was picking me up at eight and to have my bag packed. I had agreed that morning that we could spend the weekend at his place. He even offered to drop me off at the nursing home on Sunday and then pick me up again. I hadn't yet gotten around to buying that car. No time.

Dillan: Knock, knock.

I laughed when the message came through, pausing my pacing in the living room.

Me: Who's there?
Dillan: Yeah… I suck at these, but if you hurry, I have something you can suck on while we drive.

I laughed at his stupidity and picked up my bag. By the time I opened my door, he was already there.

"You took too long." He swallowed my laugh and picked me up.

My back hit the back of the door a second later. I was still wearing my dark red blouse from work. And I may or may not have unbuttoned a few extra buttons up top. Which he soon discovered as he kissed down my neck. His fingers worked on the area south of the border, while his tongue worked in the Northern district.

I was still in the coming down phase when he set me down, fixed my clothes, and then yanked me out of the apartment. I let him drag me around like a rag doll. It was faster.

I stopped, holding my ground, when I recognized the big man standing next to a black town car.

He tipped his head in greeting. My smile was shaky. "Hey, BoBo."

"Ma'am." That was it, that was all he said.

Dillan just ignored both of us as he passed my bag to BoBo, then opened the car door for me. He jumped in after me.

"Excited much?" I laughed at him.

"Yes. I like the idea of having you at my place." He leaned in and kissed me. "I may never let you leave. I told you. I like taking care of you."

And I swooned.

And apparently climbed onto his lap while I kissed him. When my senses came back to me, I was eternally grateful that I wore a skirt to work and a buttoned blouse. Even though it was now unbuttoned, only the front could be seen. So even though BoBo most likely knew what we were doing, he certainly couldn't see any of it. Not of me anyway. I was sure he would get an eyeful of Dillan if I got up.

Sensing my nerves, and probably knowing why, Dillan leaned in and kissed me again. He then whispered in my ear. "He isn't even listening to us. It's okay. I promise. Just relax. It's just you and me."

It was hard not to relax when he drew my attention like that.

Neither of us were wearing seatbelts when we arrived, or even sitting on the seat. At least I was on the seat. Laying down, but still. Dillan hovered over me, kissing me. I held onto him with my arms around his neck.

I never heard BoBo get out of the car, but he had to have, at some point.

"This whole world disappearing thing is probably not something we should encourage." I frowned at my wrinkled shirt.

"Why not?" Dillan was enjoying my annoyance too much.

"Because it isn't safe. Who knows what is going on when we are wrapped up like that?"

Dillan chuckled as he kissed my forehead and climbed out of the car. "Why do you think I asked BoBo to drive tonight? If we get distracted, he will watch our backs."

"And every other part of us." I mumbled disgruntledly.

Dillan pinched my butt then escorted me through the dark parking garage, and into an elevator. Where he cornered me.

"Anyone could walk in, ya know?"

"No, they can't. When I pushed for my penthouse, it locked the elevator. No one can get on until I am off. It's a tall building, shall we see if I can get you off before then?"

I bent down to open his pants, only to realize he had never closed them. Greedily, I dropped to my knees. "How about we get you off instead?"

I didn't give him a chance to answer. The grip on my hair was answer enough though. I was pretty sure I would have beat the elevator, but he was trying to draw it out for some reason. The doors didn't open until we finished, or rather, he did. All over my neck.

We didn't leave his apartment again until Sunday morning.

I entered the nursing home nervously, feeling like I was sneaking back into the house after curfew. Dad laughed when he saw my face.

"What did you do?"

"Nothing." I answered a little too quickly.

"Ya huh. You look like you burned the lasagna again."

I scowled at him and put my hands on my hips. "That was one time, Daddy!"

We both laughed as I walked over to where he sat on the couch. I hugged him tight.

"You smell like men's shampoo."

Oops. I pushed off the couch, creating distance as I went to find the Scrabble board. Dad had fallen in love with the game since he got to the home.

"Yeah, I spent the night at a friend's place last night and forgot to pack my own soap. He let me borrow his." Demanded more like it. Dillan got a kick out of me smelling like him.

"A friend, huh? A good friend?" I refused to look at him directly, but I could hear the teasing tone in his voice.

I huffed out a laugh. "Yes, Dad. A good friend."

"And do we like this friend?"

I dipped my head deeper and blushed. My Dad reached across the coffee table, where I was setting up the board, and patted my hand.

"I'm happy for you, Pixie." He wasn't teasing this time. He was being serious.

I lifted my head to make sure, and he seemed genuine. "Thanks, Dad. It's kind of early still, so I don't want to get my hopes up yet."

"If you are using his soap already, I'm guessing hopes have been thrown out the window for both of you. You're past that now."

My face was inflamed by the time he let us start playing. I pulled out some chicken to thaw while we played. By the time Randy arrived, it was ready to be cooked. Once again, he followed me to the kitchen.

"How've you been? I've hardly spoken to you all week."

I snorted. "Because we talked so often before?"

He cracked a smile. "Okay, I'll give you that. I was just hoping to talk to you after what happened last week. Are you okay? What happened? All you sent was a message with a thumbs up."

"Don't I look okay?"

He moved his head as he looked me over for injuries. "I guess. What was all that about with Dillan? When he came to see me, he was livid. I was terrified he was going to hurt you."

I waved his words away with my left hand. "He ticked me off, so I locked him out of his own database and accounts. He wasn't able to access anything for over a week. They had to run business the old-fashioned way. The stress had gotten to him, that's all. We worked it out, all's well now." I glanced over at Randy. He had more questions, ones I didn't want to answer. "Why don't you go hang out with Dad? Spend time with him."

Randy stared at me for another minute, then finally left. I didn't realize I was holding my breath until he was gone.

Things moved along smoothly, no more issues, until I called them to the table. They both sat down, and I carried the food over. I leaned over next to Randy, so I could set the pan of chicken in the middle of the table. I heard him sniff and expected him to say something about the food, as he usually did.

Nope.

"Why do you smell like Dillan?"

I practically dropped the chicken and ran back to the kitchen for the rice.

"Fi?" Randy called, not so happy anymore.

"Your sister stayed with a friend last night, she forgot her soap." My Dad was oh so helpful as he scooped chicken onto my plate for me.

I set the rice next to the pan and the green beans and took my seat.

"Fiona." Randy sounded distraught.

"Who says it was Dillan's soap? Anyone could have gotten it from the store."

"BS. I've heard Dillan talking about it before. He orders it online, from some place in Europe."

Dang. I forgot Dillan had said that. His stuff was awesome. I never felt so soft after. I sighed and looked at my brother.

"What's your point, Randy? You want me to admit I've been spending time with him? Fine! I see Dillan almost every day after work. Happy?"

"Fi. He's not... he's..."

"A really great guy who runs his own business, cares about me, and tries to take care of me? What's so bad about that?" I threw my napkin on the table and walked back to the kitchen. I needed a minute.

I didn't get that minute.

"Yes, he's a decent guy. But he is still a loan shark, among other things. He is involved in so many sketchy things. I'm just watching out for you. You gave him 10,000 dollars, of course he thinks you have more."

I turned and leveled him with a glare. "I gave him that to pay off *your* debt. That was because of you. You are the only person who has ever used me for money. And for your information, he gave me back all 15, and still cleared *your* debt." Ha! Swallow that pill sucker.

"Why…"

"Because he cares about me. He didn't feel right keeping my money. He also knew that money was being saved for a reason. I never told him that. He figured it out on his own. He didn't like me taking Ubers all the time. He also knows that I wouldn't allow him to buy me a car, so he gave me my money back. Dillan has way more money than me. Why would he need mine?"

"Okay, fine. It's not your money he's after. What about what you can do? He kept asking about you and computers."

I rolled my eyes and walked a few steps away from him. "I explained that to you already. I locked him out of his own company. I locked everyone out. His computer guy would have figured it out sooner or later, but Dillan was ticked that I did that. He wanted me to fix it and he didn't want to wait. Dillan has a bit of an impatience problem. At least when it comes to things involving me."

Randy winced. I laughed and patted his shoulder as I passed to leave the kitchen again. "I've never been naive, Randy. My eyes were opened to the world the moment you lost your first bet to mohawk dude."

I sat down at the table and started eating. Randy joined us a few minutes later. Dinner passed in mostly silence. Dad didn't ask what happened. But, then again, this place wasn't all that big. He may have heard it all anyway.

An hour later, we both said goodbye to our Dad, who was falling asleep on the couch.

As we stood in the elevator, I figured I would warn him. "Dillan is picking me up. Play nice."

"You know he banned me from the poker room, right? Did you have anything to do with that?"

"Yes and no. Like I said, he wants to take care of me. Which means helping you make better choices, so that I am not stressed over you. If he was really just after my money, or whatever, why would he have done that?"

"He told me you stayed the night when you went to pay him off. He made it sound like you had to because of the interest."

I laughed once as we disembarked the ride. "He offered the deal, and I slapped him. I would have stayed regardless. He just sweetened the pot. There is something about him that draws me in. He has the same response to me." I winked at Randy before I opened the lobby doors to leave. "Why do you think I locked him out digitally?"

Randy huffed, only slightly amused, and followed me out. Dillan was parked right in front of the building leaning against his blue car.

"Hey, beautiful. Have a good visit?"

I grinned and let him wrap me in his arms. "Mostly. Apparently, I smell just like you."

Dillan laughed, then kissed me in front of my brother for the first time.

"Well, that's my cue. See ya, Pixie!"

I flipped my brother off.

Dillan chuckled as he opened my door to the front seat. Once he was behind the wheel, he asked, like I knew he would. "Pixie?"

"Only my Dad calls me that. Randy only does it when he is being a butthead."

"So…"

"No!" I smacked him with the back of my hand, Dillan caught it and held it in his. "Dad only."

He gave me a mock frown. I giggled as I leaned over and kissed it.

The next month passed in a similar fashion. During the week, we stayed at my place. On the weekends, we went to Dillan's. One Saturday, I asked if he wanted to go meet my Dad. Dillan jumped at the idea. I was not expecting that response. But it did make me happy.

The two men hit it off from the beginning. Laughing, playing games. And telling stories about me. Dillan ate all of those up. Along with the cookies I made before we went there. I wouldn't let him touch them in his apartment, even though he kept trying. I slapped the back of his hand with a serving spoon, he slapped my butt harder with the same hand. Considering I had only been in one of his shirts at the time, it really hurt. He then took the spoon from me, spun me around to face him, and proceeded to use the spoon for an entirely new purpose. I would never be looking at that spoon the same way again.

We had only been there for an hour when Dillan asked to use the bathroom. Dad took that opportunity to make his opinion known.

"I like him for you." He said nonchalantly, one eye on his Scrabble tiles and one on the bathroom door.

"Good, so do I."

"He may not know it yet, but that boy is head over heels in love with you."

"Daddy!" I silently admonished him. "It's only been a month. You don't know that."

He scoffed and waved my denial away. "Please. I fell in love with your mother the moment I first laid eyes on her. It just grew stronger the more I got to know her."

I nibbled on my nails nervously. "You think?"

He smiled down to where I was sitting on the floor and patted my head softly. "Yes, Pixie. I see how he looks at you, how he always has your needs on the front of his mind." His eyes dipped to the pillow I was sitting on. Dillan had refused to let me sit on the hard floor. "You are it for him."

"But his job…"

"So what? Does a job define a person? Just because people may do bad things in his club doesn't make him a bad man. What if one of your analysts decided to hack into a bank and steal money? Would that make you a criminal too?"

I felt like he was glossing over the things we both knew Dillan was also involved in, but I got his point. I shook my head in answer.

A few hours later, as we left, my father shook Dillan's hand. "You do right by my girl, now, you hear? She deserves someone to take care of her, instead of the other way around."

Dillan wrapped his free hand, the one not being squeezed the life out of by my father, around my waist and held me close to his side. "With my life, sir."

My father nodded once, kissed me on the forehead, and shooed us out of his apartment.

As much as I would have loved to have Dillan at family dinners, I wasn't sure Randy was ready for that yet. He was growing distant again, and frequently missed dinners with Dad. I was getting worried. The only times he did that in the past was when he felt guilty about something, or he was focused on a new play.

There was a time I would have obsessed over it, nagging to find out what he was doing. But I was enjoying my life too much to let the stress of Randy's life bother me. I trusted Dillan to do what he could to keep Randy straight.

And, for once, I just wanted to enjoy my life and not worry about my older brother.

A little over two months after Dillan and I became official, I once again met with a potential new client and one of the Senior Partners.

"Miss Reynolds, I'd like you to meet Ivan Smirnov. He runs a chain of hotels and sports bars here in Los Angeles." Gary waved a hand toward the man standing near him in the conference room.

I walked over and offered my hand. "Mr. Smirnov, it's a pleasure to meet you."

His hand was rough and calloused, but he did not squeeze too hard. I was grateful for that, because he looked like he could break my hand with one shake.

"Call me Ivan, Miss Reynolds." His accent was thick, but I didn't know where from. The down side to life behind a computer.

I smiled sweetly at him, hiding the fact that he gave me the creeps. It had been a while since I tried so hard to hide my true feelings. It felt weird. I also had to keep myself from wondering when I had let my guard down so completely.

"Fiona then."

"Ah, a beautiful name. Irish for fair. I must say, I agree this case."

I tipped my head slightly - acknowledging but not thanking him - in his direction, then looked over and Gary shook his hand.

"Gary, I haven't had the pleasure of working with you much. Lawerence usually handles my neck of the woods." Gary gave me a knowing smile. I shook my head and smiled. "I see." He was just as curious as his counterparts. Got it.

"Ivan has a different kind of problem he wants to discuss today. I usually handle this side of the business. And I must say, I was curious to see your talents at work. I hear they are a thing of beauty."

Called it.

I laughed and strolled over to the other side of the table, waving my hand for where Ivan and his man should sit. "Only in our world would it be considered a thing of beauty."

Gary shrugged and sat next to me. Once everyone was seated, I began the meeting.

"So, tell me Ivan, what can we do for you today? What kind of services are you needing?"

"We believe we had intrusion. A week ago, our system start acting funny. Things slow, some things could no be accessed, etc. Now, we have in-house tech team. They believe we have virus. That we may been hacked, but they fail find culprit. We heard your firm would be help with that."

I opened my laptop, the one Linda had already set on the table for me, along with my coffee – she spoiled me - and started typing. "That should be easy to find out. Did your tech team narrow down the specific places they think were hacked?"

The two men looked at each other. The unknown man shrugged his shoulders.

"No, they did not."

Okay, unknown was on the tech team, or at least involved with them.

"That's not a problem, it would have just helped me know where to start. What was being done on the computers when the problem first started?"

Ivan gave a helpless look. "We have many employees, much work done at once…"

I nodded. I hacked into the administration mainframe. "Any specific location I should be looking into, or all locations on the same VPN? Or WAN?"

Ivan looked at the silent man again, almost like he was looking for a translation.

"VPN." The man answered again, without an accent I noticed. "The problem seems to be spreading, but it started in one of our sports bars near San Fernando."

I nodded and typed away for a minute. I pulled up the database for The Perun Hotel. It had a sports bar connected to the lobby. Separate entrances were available, for non-hotel guests. Perun, from what a side search told me, was basically the Russian version of Zeus and a bit of Aries. He ruled the other gods with lightning and thunder. He blessed the people, but he was also the god of war. Something about that name seemed significant, I just couldn't put my finger on why yet.

There was a folder marked Game Night, so I clicked on it. I kept myself from rolling my eyes. A bookie folder. They had gambling there. Awesome.

I strolled through, but nothing seemed amiss. No sign of a virus. In fact, they had a very secure system. It shouldn't have been so easy for me to get in. It was almost like they were holding back their defenses, lulling me into a false sense of security.

A weight of doom settled over me when that thought hit me.

I looked up at Ivan, who was watching me expectantly. I opened a few cameras, getting a look at the place.

I stopped when I came across a man who looked to be sleeping in one of the stock rooms. Only, it wasn't actually a stock room. It was too empty. It also didn't look like it belonged inside a hotel.

A basement perhaps?

Or a warehouse…

I ran a back trace to see where the footage was coming from. Sure enough, this feed had been fed in. I was right, they wanted me to see this.

I zoomed in and got a better look at the man.

"Ah, I think you have an issue with one of your employees. He seems to be confusing a stock room with a hotel room. It looks like he has been there for some time. He may be living there, most likely temporarily. Until he can get back on his feet."

Ivan grinned. "I wondered if he move in. He never seem to leave. Practically live in sports bar. He access anything else?"

You wanna play this game? Fine. Let's play. "I do not believe so. Although your system was a breeze to get through. Anybody could have hacked into it. The virus was probably just him trying to cover his tracks. Distraction, as it were, while he settled in somewhere. I would keep an eye on things at the sports bar though. Desperate men do desperate things."

"They do, at that. I be honored if you come for lunch today, let me thank you, and get opinion on upping defenses."

I turned to Gary, who was grinning like a proud papa.

"By all means. Go. Sometimes we can get more information when we are closer to the problem."

I raised an incredulous eyebrow and he laughed. "Alright, *most* people get more information when they are closer." He stood and shook his head with laughter. "Such a treat."

I didn't even do much that was impressive this time. Especially since this was all a trick. A game to these men. I wasn't sure who they were exactly, but I wasn't naïve.

I smiled tightly to the men, rethinking my opinion on who the silent man was. "Just let me instruct my secretary to move my next meeting and cancel my lunch. Then I will be free to go."

Ivan and his little friend stood with me. The friend followed me out the door and to my office. Awesome.

Linda was not at her desk when I walked over. I mentally cursed. I walked into my office and traded my laptop for my purse, locking the desk drawer to keep it safe. I picked up a post-it and a pen.

"What are you doing?"

"My secretary has already gone to lunch it seems, so I am leaving instructions on what I need her to do." I answered the man.

He walked around my desk to stand next to me, looking over my shoulder.

Last minute lunch meeting. Please call Mrs. Weber and cancel lunch. Apologize profusely. Tell her we will discuss her problem with Dill Pill later. Reschedule my afternoon meetings, as I will be on site at...

"No." The man roughly grabbed my arm, leaving a line on the paper. "Do not tell her where you are going. I'm sure I don't need to say why."

I huffed. "Sorry. I'm used to online cloak and dagger games, not in person."

I picked up the note. His little addition would help anyway. I was sure Dillan would figure everything else out, including what that line meant.

I hoped so at any rate. As I said, I wasn't used to the in-person version of this.

I walked out of the room and set the note on her desk, where she would see it. I wished I could do more.

As we walked toward the elevators, and Ivan, Chris came out of his office. I had a light bulb moment. It was always better to carry more than one parachute, just in case.

I walked over and leaned in. He automatically kissed my cheek like we did before. "Sorry I have to miss lunch with you and Mrs. Weber. I left instructions for Linda to cancel. I have a business lunch I can't miss. See you later?"

Chris smiled, and moved a hair behind my ear, playing along beautifully. "Sure. Although she is probably going to be upset with you."

I waved it away with a scoff. "She can handle Dill on her own. She should just fire him already instead of constantly trying to trap him."

"It's kind of hard to fire your lover." He laughed.

I smirked, thank you for the opening. "Nah, just lock them out of their own company. Works every time." I winked and stepped back.

Gary waved goodbye as I stepped up to Ivan, he had probably been trying to keep the new "client" company.

"Shall we?" Ivan put his hand up to hold the elevator doors for me. For once, the ride was empty of other occupants. "Who was that man?"

"A friend and co-worker. He has been showing interest, and I have been keeping my options open."

"Do you have a lot of experiences with lovers and locking them out of their own company?"

"Yes, on both accounts. I find it is the best way to deal with liars and cheats. None of mine of course. Well, not the lovers' part. Just the liars and cheats. I vet my lovers better than that."

Ivan and his man laughed. "I wish we were meeting under better circumstances, Fiona. What a wonderful partnership we would have had. Alas, I think that ship has sailed."

I pressed my lips together and nodded tightly.

I was going to kill Randy when this was over. He never listens.

Chapter 11

Dillan

I closed my eyes and mentally prayed for patience as two hands came up from behind me, sliding around my waist. The slender body slowly made its way to my side. There was a time I would have lifted my arm for her and held her to me. Never out of a desire to hold her, more out of habit. A habit I thought we had put an end to.

I stood perfectly still as Bunny moved to my front. I leaned back when her lips made for my jaw. She pouted.

"What's wrong?"

I moved my arms enough to grasp both of her upper arms and push her off me. "How many times have we been through this, Bunny? I said no more. You can talk to me like a regular person, without being all over me. My girlfriend has a problem with it, and so do I, frankly."

She scoffed and folded her arms.

"What do you need?" There weren't even any customers here yet. We had hours until we opened.

She purred and tried coming closer again. I stepped back. "I need you. I miss you."

I raised a hand between us. She stopped but tried to grab my hand. That obviously wasn't going to happen.

"No, Bunny. You know better. Keep this up, and you will be looking for a new job."

Bunny scowled at me, but thankfully dropped the act. "All this because some hoe that doesn't belong in our world impressed you by locking you out of your own company? She came to pay off her brother's debt. She is just with you for your money. When are you going to see that?"

I pointed sternly at the locker room door, where the dancers got ready. She stomped her way there, growling like a put-out cat.

I sighed and rubbed my head.

Wayne, one of my security guards, jogged over a few moments later, looking stressed. "Sir, we have a situation up front."

This day was really not getting off to a good start. "What is it?"

He turned to walk back toward the front entrance, so I followed. "There is a woman there screaming that she needs to get in and see you. She kept saying all sorts of stuff that didn't make sense. Something about a secretary named Linda, a note about canceling a lunch that was never planned and dealing with a Dill Pill. It wasn't until she said something about a Fi that BoBo sent me to get you."

I almost tripped over my feet as I came to a sudden stop. I repeated everything he had said, in my head. Then I took off running. I rushed through the front door and found a frantic pregnant woman standing on the front steps of my club.

"Are you Dillan?" She was practically begging for me to be.

"Yes. Who are you? What happened to Fiona? Is she safe?"

That was it, that was all it took. The woman fell to pieces as she rambled.

"I don't know. I'm Katia, her best friend." I nodded that I knew of her, and she continued. "I got a call from Linda about an hour ago. Linda is…"

"Fiona's secretary, yes."

Katia sighed like me knowing anything about Fi was a relief. "When she got back from lunch, Chris, another junior partner at the firm, told her that Fi had given him some cryptic message about canceling lunch, locking lovers out of their own company, and then told her that Fi left a note for her before she went on a business lunch. Linda recognized the story about you, so she rushed to the desk and found the note. It basically told her to call me and cancel lunch. We didn't have one scheduled, so I was confused. Until she told me the note said I would have to deal with Dill Pill on my own. I figured that meant you."

I worked to keep my breathing steady. I needed to stay calm, not freak out. "Did Fiona say where she was going?"

"No, but Linda said that it looked like she was about to, but there was a strange line instead. She doesn't know what it means." Katia hiccupped. "I tried calling her, but it went straight to voicemail every time. Where is Fi? What's going on?"

"If I had to guess, Fiona's worst fear. Someone has found her and taken her." I patted her shoulder, trying to be comforting, but I had never met the woman. I didn't know what she would find comforting. Plus, I was still new to the emotional game. A freaked out pregnant woman was way beyond my capabilities.

"Go home, wait there. Don't put any extra stress on your body. Fiona would be very upset if anything happened to you or your babies. I will find her and bring her home." And lock her up. "I promise."

Katia nodded before falling against me for a hug. I warily patted her back and then she took off.

"Katia, wait!" She turned back around. "Where does she work? I need to start from the beginning."

She rattled off an address and a company name.

I spun and ran for my car, Bobo right next to me.

"Orders, sir?"

"Get me there as fast as possible."

"Yes, sir." We both jumped through our own doors at the same time.

I called Keith from the car and filled him in.

I expected the trip to take longer, but BoBo, whether he would admit it or not, was worried about Fiona.

He pulled up to the side of the building and I jumped out. I knew he would join me as soon as the car was parked properly.

I rudely shoved my way through the elevator queue and pushed in through the doors.

"Sir, we do not act so rashly here."

I glanced at one of the many men in suits. Pushing back the urge to curse him out or just slug him - Fiona would have been upset with me since this might be a co-worker - I kept my composure.

"Normally, I wouldn't, but this is an emergency."

He huffed and lifted his head to look at the numbers as they passed by. I swear it took ages to reach the 14th floor. The man grumbled again when the doors opened, and I pushed my way through.

I stalled at the front desk. I looked at the company name long enough to register the cyber security portion, everything else didn't matter. The receptionist was on the phone, and every time I tried to get her attention, she lifted a finger. I chose to ignore the fact that the elevator man literally stood in the hall watching me curiously.

"Screw this." I mumbled, walking around the desk.

The woman finally hung up the phone in a hurry, trying to chase after me. "Sir, sir, you can't just walk back here like this."

I stopped again, looking around for some sign to direct me. The room was too wide, and there were too many cubicles in the middle. I didn't have time for this. *Fiona* didn't have time for this.

"Linda!" I shouted. The room froze as the receptionist caught up to me.

"Sir…"

"Dillan?" I turned toward another woman, one who looked nearly as frazzled as Katia had.

"Where is she? What happened?"

"I don't know." She waved for me to follow her and led me to one of the side offices. She bent down and picked up a wrinkled note while telling me the same story Katia had.

I studied the note carefully. The harsh line at the bottom made my stomach bottom out. I crumpled the note in fury.

"Someone kept her from saying where she was going."

Linda must have already known this, but hearing it made her collapse into her chair in tears.

"What's going on?" The man, who had obviously taken up following me, asked. At least this time he seemed more worried than irritated.

I turned to look at him, wondering if he would be of any help. I noticed a younger man looking nervous as he stood off to the side. I pointed at him.

"Chris?" He nodded. "What did Fiona say before she left?"

He repeated it back nearly verbatim, as though he had been reciting it in his head to make sure he got the message right.

From the corner of my eye, I saw the elevator man getting confused. "She went to lunch with a client and was going to check out his system. What's the big deal? We do this all the time."

My anger turned on him and he flinched. "Fiona is missing, that is the big deal. She left a trail of clues behind, informing her secretary to get a hold of me."

"And exactly who are you?" He didn't seem to quite believe me yet.

"Her boyfriend." I spat through my teeth.

The man opened his mouth and then closed it, not sure what to say to that. I noticed that Chris looked a little glum. That was telling.

"I have connections she didn't want the firm to know about. She loves her job. Now tell me about this client."

"He, uh," the elevator man licked his lips nervously, finally starting to catch up. "He requested a meeting, said he thought someone hacked his system."

"You were in the meeting?"

"Yes, finding culprits is my domain. I asked for Fiona's help because I wanted to see her in action."

I smirked. "She is the best. What happened next?" We were drawing a crowd, but I didn't care.

"She used her computer to access his database. She said it didn't look like anything had been tampered with, but an employee may be living at work. They didn't seem surprised by this. They asked if they could take her to lunch at the bar in the hotel, and then get her opinion on tightening things up."

I rubbed my hands through my hair. "What's the name of the client?"

"Ivan Smirnov."

I huffed, which slowly turned into maniacal laughter. The two men took a step back. "Don't you morons vet your clients before meeting with them?"

"We… we did. He owns a chain of hotels."

I bent over, holding my head as I shook it. Then I stood up and looked straight into his eyes. "He also runs the local Bratva syndicate. Fiona got kidnapped by the Russian mafia right in front of you."

Linda gasped from behind me, and Chris paled.

"How do you know that?" The elevator man, who was obviously a Senior Partner in the firm, and therefore her boss, partially whispered.

I threw out both my arms to the side. "Because I run a club downtown. The mafia frequent it. As long as I give them their space, they leave me and my club alone. I have no desire for them to take over my very lucrative business."

I rubbed my eyes again, right as BoBo walked onto the floor. He watched me warily as he came to stand next to me. The others all took more than one step back. The man certainly carried a presence.

"Sir?" He waited for instructions.

"Ivan has her. He posed as a client. Somehow Fiona knew something was wrong. Maybe she saw something on the computer. I need Jorge to hack her computer, see if he can find what it was."

"I can do it. I may not be as good as Fiona, but I know what I am doing." Chris gulped when my eyes settled on him. "And I'm already here."

He made a good point. "Fine. Do it." I looked back at BoBo, silently telling him to still make the call.

Linda picked up a key and walked into the closed office. "She locks it in her desk."

Our whole group moved inside. BoBo stayed outside the door, guarding, and making the calls for me.

Linda knelt behind the desk and unlocked it. She set the laptop down on the desk, where Chris was already sitting on the visitor side. I took a minute to look around the office. There wasn't much in the way of decorations. Just the basics. Her degree, and a few pictures. There was one with Katia and her family. One of Fiona with her Dad and brother.

Then another one. One that made me pause.

I picked it up and nearly started crying myself. That one picture was nearly my undoing.

Here she talked about keeping our relationship a secret, and she had a picture of us sitting on her desk. It was during one of the few times I managed to convince her to go somewhere with me.

We had driven all the way to Ventura and spent the day on the beach. Fiona had laughed as I took the selfie of us sitting on a blanket together. She was in my arms, where she was safest. I never sent her a copy of it, but then, I wouldn't have to. If Fiona wanted something digital, she got it herself.

"She never really got over the guilt of keeping you a secret." Linda said softly, sniffling. "She was trying to think of a way to blend the two best parts of her life."

I cursed, that about did me end right there, and looked up at the lights, blinking. That little brat.

BoBo stepped into the office. His look said he wanted to say something but wasn't sure with mixed company. He knew as well as I did how private Fiona was. I nodded my permission and set the picture back in its spot.

"Sir, could this be related to Randy?"

My eyebrows slowly lowered. I hadn't thought about the why yet. I was mostly stuck on the where. I started to pull my phone back out of my pocket, but BoBo spoke again, making that unnecessary.

"Keith already has someone looking for him."

"Who is Randy?" The Senior Partner asked.

"Her brother. He's a degenerate gambler. Fiona has done her best to keep him at arm's length from her life. But she loves him and has bailed him out one too many times. It's how we met, actually."

He hummed, not looking pleased at all.

"Who her brother has turned out to be is not her fault. She has done everything she could to keep her work and personal life separate. Her own brother doesn't even know where she lives or works. They meet in a mutual location. I didn't even know where she worked until her best friend brought me the message from Linda. I'm very curious to know how Ivan figured it out."

"I got it!" Chris shouted. "She has a lot of security on her computer, but I got in. I have a feeling she did that on purpose though."

I rushed over to him. "Can you access her history?"

"Don't need to. She left it all open." He turned the computer around in his hands to show me. "That man doesn't look like he is sleeping in a stock room." He added in a horrified whisper.

"That's because that is a warehouse, and he is tied up. That is also her brother. They planted that video footage for her. They were subtly telling her they had him. Any chance you can backtrace that to find her?"

Chris shook his head sadly. "No. That was always Fiona's side of things when she worked for me. At least on people who cover up this deeply."

"I can." A new voice said from the door. I breathed a sigh of relief when I saw him standing next to BoBo. "I heard through the grapevine that you might need me. Thankfully, I was already downtown seeing a play. I've been studying everything Fiona did to our system. She keeps adding things too, like she is teaching me."

"What? She still has access? Why didn't you tell me?" Chris and I moved so Jorge could take the laptop.

He shrugged. "She was helping me secure your interests better. I thought that was a good thing. And her tricks are very intriguing. I can't wait to finally meet her." He took his eyes off the computer, where his fingers were still flying over the keyboard. "I do finally get to meet her, right? Now that you basically announced your relationship to the world?"

I huffed a small laugh. Jorge was still besotted with her. If not more now. "Yes, as soon as we bring her home."

Chapter 12

Fiona

"Where is Randy?" I demanded, the moment we were driving on the road.

"He is safe. For now." Ivan sat across from me in their… limo?

I wasn't really sure what it was. It had extra seats in the back, but it wasn't all that long. From the outside it kind of looked like a regular town car, just a bit longer.

"What did you do to him?"

Ivan clicked his tongue a few times while shaking his head. "You are not one who is in charge, Fiona." He said my name slowly, dragging it out.

"No, but you want something from me and I'm not doing diddly until I know Randy is okay. So… what did you do to him?"

Both of the men chuckled, as did the driver.

"We asked him few questions, is all. He was no forthcoming in beginning, but he come around. Now he sleeping off."

I looked out the car window, trying to keep my face impassive while inside my heart was breaking. I warned the idiot. I told him something like this would eventually happen. Did he listen? Obviously not.

"How much does he owe you?"

"Enough that I don't think you be paying this one back on your own. This time we are going to do in trade."

I turned to face him, giving him a "you've got me kidding me" look. He laughed and waved both hands in the air.

"No thing like that, I assure you… well, no unless you misbehave. As I saw in conference room, you have many, many talents, Ms. Reynolds. All of which will no only settle brother's debt, also settle debt of my own." His voice deepened into a dark drawl by the end. It gave me goosebumps. And not the kind Dillan's deep commanding voice gave me.

"I'm not doing anything until I see Randy for myself. I need to see that he is alive. After that, I will help you. Just this once. And then you will let us both go."

Ivan gave me a patronizing look. "We see what happens."

In other words, it didn't matter. They were going to kill us anyway. The least I could do was drag this out, giving the grapevine enough time to get to Dillan. I had to trust that Dillan would save me. I had to believe he cared for me as much as I did him.

I had to believe that my father was right.

It took nearly an hour before we pulled up to a warehouse on the other side of LA. I waited quietly as they parked and let me out of the car. Then I followed Ivan into the building, the other man following behind me. We walked down a narrow corridor, passing many rooms with closed doors. We stopped outside the last one.

A guard stood sentinel in the hall, next to the door. When he saw us, he opened the door and waved for me to go in. With my arms folded, trying not to let any of them get close enough to touch me, I warily walked inside. When I saw Randy curled up on the floor, I immediately ran over and dropped next to him, looking for a pulse.

He was beaten black and blue. Worse than when Dillan had made him fight off the debt.

I checked for a pulse in his neck, releasing a breath when I felt the faint beat. I dropped my head to his.

"What did you do this time, you idiot?"

The men chuckled from where they stood at the wall. "He made many large bets, both on sports games at bar, and poker games in back. What he win at table, he lost in bar." Ivan explained. "I heard he supposed be cut off. I assume you terrify Dillan with little trick."

My head snapped to him. How the hell did he know about that? What else did he know?

He grinned. "Dillan so angry when you cut him off. And then he took out on his poor employees. I often enjoy company of one. She all too ready vent her frustrations slightest opportunity. It was easy pry her for more information after. A woman scorned really is best tool against untouchable adversary. She told me all about how you storm way into club, demanding speak Dillan. And they all just cater to you. She so angry when she find out what you did to him. And yet, he no punish you. Instead, he help you. It make me wonder what you find on him. What you did with that information."

"I did nothing. He's a lying, cheating, dirtbag. He forced my brother to fight, won a boatload of money off him, and then still insisted we pay more. Dillan deserved what he got. I only gave him back access because he promised not to let my brother back in. He promised he would spread the word around town."

Ivan put a hand to his heart, like he felt for me. "An honorable thing to do, but, unfortunately, Dillan can no control rest of us. He a powerful man, sure. But he can no control deals we each make. To be fair, I was curious after my little bunny tell me. I remember your brother. See, it was my man who fought him in ring. Dillan consistently refuses my offers to work together, but he still take my money when comes to fights. I no want partnership anymore. I want control of *Indecent*. Of his poker room and fighting rings. When he first opened it no problem. I did no think he would go far. I since learn I was wrong. His power grow all time. He has stayed in his lane, yes, but I will no allow anyone to have more power than me. Los Angeles is my domain. And with your help I can take out two adversaries for price of one."

I was lost on what all he was talking about.

"Dillan no much of a problem, more like annoying thorn in shoe. I prefer him be under my umbrella. The Italians, now they problem. I want you make look like they coming after Dillan. Make so he has no choice but seek aid from me."

"Which you will offer, with a deal of your own." I deadpanned back.

Ivan grinned back at me. "Yes."

With a dramatic sigh, I sat on the floor, keeping a protective hand on Randy's shoulder. "What do you want me to do?"

"Nothing you have no done before. I want you break into Dillan's system. Transfer funds from Italians. Make look like someone in Dillan's organization paying bribes to them. Plant evidence on Italian's side, like they trying forcefully take over *Indecent*."

"And where do you want the Italian funds to go?" Like I really had to ask.

"Me of course. Make them think Dillan stealing their money."

"You're basically asking me to start a war between Dillan and the Italians." I needed to be positive here.

He seemed pleased that I caught that. "Yes, exactly. Dillan no equip fight war against Italian mafia. He need help. My help. Which come at price."

"Why me? Why Randy?"

He shrugged. "Your brother showing up was fate. I need someone who could do all this. Bunny no know your name. But I knew Randy's face. I knew what you do. I figure you already had… beef with Dillan, so you willing take him down." He waved towards my unconscious brother. "He just insurance policy."

"Right." I pushed myself backward until I was leaning against the wall. "Let's get started shall we, I have a date tonight. I will need a computer."

Ivan laughed and snapped his fingers. The silent man took the bag off his shoulders, one I hadn't noticed before, and brought it to me.

"Don't try to do anything sneaky, I will know if you do."

My smile was sardonic as I looked at him. "What makes you think I'd try anything like that?"

"Do and you are both dead." He warned.

I gave him a mocked shiver, as though I was saying I was so scared. He scowled and walked out of the room. The guard from outside pulled a chair in through the open doorway and sat down.

"Neil monitor you. No try anything. You do, I may change mind on which talents of yours I put use." Ivan winked, then walked out.

I quickly opened the computer, there was no need to log in. Morons. I quickly found their screen recorder, where they would watch everything I was doing. I opened a new tab and kept it secret in a small corner. In that corner, I cast a remote login code and took over my own work laptop. As expected, someone was on it. I reversed things and made it so they could watch me.

Chapter 13

Dillan

Gary, after finally introducing himself, left to go take care of his own business. He expressly demanded I keep him updated. Chris left silently not long after. Linda was sitting at her desk, biting her nails. Me on the other hand, I was pacing a hole in the floor.

All under the watchful eye of BoBo.

We both nearly jumped when Jorge started laughing.

"What? What's going on?" Linda came running back in.

"I just fell in love, that's what. This woman, I just don't know what to do with her."

I growled at my techie.

He lifted a hand, not even looking at me. "Chill, Dill Pill."

I grunted and rolled my eyes. "Don't ever call me that again. Now what happened."

"Fiona is online, she made it so I can watch her. This will make it a lot easier to track her. The video feed is being bounced all over the place. I can do it, but she may be somewhere else by then."

I moved to stand behind him and see for myself. I had no clue what was going on, I just saw the mouse and screen moving all on its own.

"What's she doing?" I asked curiously. "Wait… that's my system. Those are my bank accounts!"

"Yep." Jorge pointed to another corner. "And that looks like Bruno's. What you got going on little mouse?"

We watched as Fiona worked to break passwords on the Italian side, it was more difficult than mine. But then again, all of my stuff was in English.

"What game is Ivan playing?" I whispered.

A small picture popped up on the screen, bombs going off.

"War." BoBo said from behind me. "Ivan is trying to start a war."

Yeah, that made sense.

Another picture quickly followed. Oliver Twist begging for food. Rapidly followed by the Russian flag.

"And Ivan thinks I will come to him for help." I tskd. "Do you think he knows who she is to me?"

"No. He would have forced your hand instead of taking other tactics." BoBo grunted.

The last picture was the most confusing. It was of a bunny rabbit wearing a black mask and carrying a magnifying glass.

"What the hell does that mean?" I nearly shouted.

"Looks like a bunny being sneaky." Jorge giggled. "Bunny spy."

My eyes met BoBo's. "Call Keith, tell him to grab Bunny and hold her." I pulled out my own phone and stepped away from the desk. "Keep working on that trace, Jorge."

"Haven't stopped. What are you going to do?"

"I'm doing what she said. I'm calling for help. Just not the people who are expecting me." I put the phone to my ear and waited out the numerous rings.

"I don't remember you ever actually using this number. What's going on?" Bruno answered, his accent not nearly as thick as Ivan's.

"I'm calling in a favor."

"I don't owe you any favors."

I grinned. "Not that you admitted as much, but we both know I saved you from a pretty little cop."

He sighed. "I was hoping you forgot about that. Not my proudest moment."

"I had actually, until Ivan Smirnov kidnapped my girlfriend and is trying to start a war between you and me."

The other line was silent for a moment, but the tension coming through the waves let me know he was still there.

"How do you know all this?"

"Because he doesn't know she is my girlfriend. And he made the mistake of giving a computer to a known hacker."

Bruno laughed. "And how are we going to play with our food today?"

"That's where I need your help. We almost have a lock on their location. You know I stick to my own side of the road. I never deviate. This is my first time dealing with something like this." I explained what we believed the plan was. "I need your help."

"Yes, and it seems this is going to be mutually beneficial. I will pull the manpower together. You get me that location and I will take care of the rest."

"I'm coming with you."

He huffed, or was it a sigh? "I had a feeling as much. I take it this girlfriend is not a temporary thing?"

"No." I didn't even have to think about that. Fiona had never been temporary for me. I hung up with him and turned back to Jorge. "Anything?"

"They have some kind of blocker on their location. I tried to access it on her computer, through the remote she set up. But she digitally slapped my hand." He chuckled again, sounding like he was having the time of his life. "Absolutely love this woman."

"You do remember who she belongs to right?"

Jorge snorted. "Yes. Besides, I'm head over heels in love with my boyfriend."

"You're gay!" BoBo practically shouted from the doorway, on his way back in. "But I've seen you making out with chicks!"

Jorge laughed with a shrug, his fingers not once deviating from the keyboard. How the hell did he do that?

"I wasn't always gay. Not until I showed up at the club one night. It only took one look, a few words, and… I don't know. At first, I thought I had just met my best friend. We went out after work that night, and he kissed me. My first reaction was a bit of a freak-out, the next, not so much. Turns out there is such a thing as love at first sight. Who knew?"

"I get it. I felt the same way when Fiona walked up to my table that night. The urge to touch her, to be near her, was overpowering."

They both laughed at me.

"Hence the lie to get her to stay." Jorge teased.

"Yes, but it was just a cover. We both knew it, but we both also wouldn't admit it."

"Hence the little hack job." BoBo murmured.

I grinned. "I was so mad all week that I had completely forgotten the pull. It only took one look in her eyes for me to remember." I swallowed the growing emotions. "I can't go back to not having her. As soon as Ivan is done with her, he will either kill her, or keep her until she wishes she were dead."

"Well, I can't give you an exact location, but I can give you the whereabouts." Jorge finally broke eye contact with the computer screen. "They are in a warehouse on the South side of the city."

Without a word, I turned and walked out Fiona's office door. They both followed, Jorge still holding her work computer open in front of him. It was the only link we had.

"News?" Linda begged from her desk. I hadn't even realized she had gone back to it.

"We're getting closer. We have a general location. I will have Fiona call you as soon as she is safe."

Linda nodded numbly and sat back down. Chris looked up from his desk, his office door open. He didn't say anything and neither did I. I was in a hurry.

Jorge and I slid into my backseat while BoBo jumped in the front. Sitting still wasn't working for me, so I called Keith.

"Do you have Bunny?"

"Yes. She's in the studio acting like she is the Queen of the castle. What's going on?"

"Fiona was able to make contact. I believe they are having her work off Randy's debt. That's what makes the most sense. She managed to send us a message of sorts. One of them sounds like she was calling Bunny a spy. Ivan is a favorite client of hers, she may have said things she wasn't supposed to. Care to get her to talk?"

Keith snorted. "Not really, but I will. There is only one way that works with her."

I grinned. "Well, we did say you needed to find your own entertainment."

I could picture his grimace perfectly. He thought she was hot, but her personality tended to turn him off. I was sure Ivan had used the same methods Keith was about to. But Ivan probably enjoyed it more.

I spent the rest of the drive, after messaging Bruno where we were headed, just staring out the window. My mind flew back to that perfect weekend in Ventura.

Chapter 14

Dillan

By the time Fiona pulled into her parking garage, with her new little Toyota Corolla - because it was just her, so why did she need a bigger or fancier car - I had a bag packed for her and stowed in the trunk of my Aviator.

"Hey, beautiful." I greeted her in the lobby. If she went up to her apartment, we'd probably never leave. And not just because of her.

"Hello yourself, handsome." She grinned as she leaned in and kissed me.

Over her shoulder, I saw the security guard shaking his head with silent laughter. It was better than the worry he had a few moments ago. Someone had been spotted watching the building. He had a picture of the guy and wanted me to know. Eventually I would tell Fiona that her brother had found her. I figured he probably followed her home from dinner on Sunday. Now that she had her own car, she could get home on her own.

I frequently kicked myself for that one. I liked giving Fiona rides. The best times were when we were stuck in traffic on the freeway. My girl didn't like people watching, but she enjoyed the thrill of hiding and nearly getting caught. And I enjoyed the things she did to me while I drove.

"What are you doing down here? Are you leaving?" She frowned. Her dislike of me leaving always filled me with this weird light, happy feeling.

"No." I brushed my hands through her beautiful brown hair. "I was waiting for you."

"Down here? In the lobby?"

I kissed her forehead and smiled. "Yes, I don't trust myself to leave again when the bed is close by."

Fiona went on her toes to whisper in my ear. "Since when did we need a bed for that?"

I snagged her hand and pulled her toward the exit, making both the security guard and the doorman laugh. "On that note, we need to get moving."

"Where are we going?" Fiona laughed happily, moving faster to wrap her arms around my back. I slowed my walk so she wouldn't fall. I enjoyed her there, her arms holding me.

My car was parked out front, something the doorman had let me do, frequently. "I'm taking you out on a real date."

Fiona paused, one foot in the door. "Dillan..."

I put a finger over her lips, reminding myself that she wasn't ashamed of who I was. This was just part of who she was. "I'm taking you out of the city, someplace I doubt we will run into anybody. I've worked it all out. Trust me? Please."

Fiona put a hand on my cheek and kissed the other. "I do trust you. It's the rest of the world I don't trust."

I kissed her head one more time and helped her into the car. "I know, princess."

Not for the first time over the last few weeks, I cursed Randy out in my head.

Fiona wrapped herself around my right arm, laying her head on my shoulder, as I pulled into traffic. I listened as she told me about her day. I loved hearing her laugh about anything. I loved how happy she was when she talked about her job. She told me about the hacker they caught today. The client thought for sure it was some big conspiracy. It turned out it was his son. Who was bored with the low-level job he had been given within the company. He had made it through the firewalls that blocked certain sites in the office. While the tech team was frantically searching for who broke in, he had broken out. The client was completely embarrassed about it all. Understandably.

Next, she told me about the appointment she went to with Katia. Andy couldn't make it to the ultrasound because one of the girls was home sick today. They couldn't find anyone else willing to be with a sick toddler. Katia always got nervous in ultrasounds. So, Fiona volunteered to go with her.

While she talked about the growth of the twin boys, who were just about four months along, I began picturing Fiona with a rounded belly. I imagined putting my ear to her stomach, trying to hear the faint heartbeat. I could see me holding her hand while we got pictures of our son or daughter. I heard our laughter in my head when the baby would kick me through her stomach. I could practically feel the weight of the small bundle in my arms, as I sat next to a sweaty but happy Fiona. I imagined the exhaustion as I pulled myself out of bed to change a dirty diaper so Fiona could catch up on some sleep.

My eyes widened when I realized what I was doing. It was one thing to know I never wanted to lose the woman next to me. It was another entirely to be planning a life, a family, with her. I had never planned on having a family. Ever.

What the hell did she do to me? And why didn't I want it to stop?

"So, can you tell me where you are taking me now?" Fiona's eyes glittered with her smile.

She was happy, she was relaxed – the way she always was with me. Whatever she was doing to me, I was doing the same for her. That was comforting at least.

I smiled down at her. "No, not yet. It's a surprise."

"Hmm, I do love surprises." Her left hand left my arm and slid onto my thigh.

I cleared my throat, but my voice still came out croaky. "Yeah, how much?"

"This much." Her hand rubbed me over my pants. And my pants tightened.

Now, this reaction to her I understood.

My hands tightened on the wheel when she was no longer on the outside of my clothing. "You're going to cause us to crash if you keep this up."

We weren't sitting in bumper-to-bumper traffic this time. We were going 80 down an open freeway with a dozen other cars.

"Are you saying you want me to stop?"

"Hell, no!" I half shouted.

She giggled and gripped me tighter before shifting her position, replacing her hand with something much better. And cleaner. Less mess this way.

I moved my right hand off the steering wheel and slid it down the back of her slacks. Well, I tried to at any rate, they were a bit tight. Until they suddenly loosened. Fiona had unbuttoned them for me and was kind enough to push them down to her knees. Her pants weren't the only things to go down either. Her perfect butt was bare and smooth as I grabbed it with my hand. And then smacked it.

I hissed as she went harder on me. I smacked her a few more times before moving my hand under her, towards the front. She couldn't move her legs far apart, but I was able to lean over just enough to reach what I wanted. I ended up having to release her when I got close to the edge. I gripped her hair, keeping her head in place as I lifted and shoved into her, Like the good little girl she was, she took every last drop.

Fiona fell onto my lap a minute later, her breathing heavy, a smile on her face. I made a loop in the air with my finger, and she rolled over onto her back. Her shirt was already open for me as well. While I drove, I kept one eye on her and one eye on the road, as my hand played with the various parts she was leaving open for me. It was only fair since she hadn't exactly covered me back up either.

It was a good thing there weren't as many cars on this part of the highway. My driving wasn't as straight and even as it normally would have been at these speeds.

I wasn't surprised in the least bit when Fiona fell asleep. My girl was usually pretty tired by Friday. I let her sleep, and even did up most of the buttons on her shirt. I meant to do all of them, but I really didn't want to close the curtains on the best view in the world.

We only got stuck behind one accident, which nearly doubled our travel time, but it gave her plenty of time to rest. It also gave me an opportunity to carefully lean over and move her pants back up. She lifted her waist enough to allow me to do so. I worried she would wake up completely, but she sank back deeper once that was done.

I woke Fiona when we pulled up to a small beach house in Ventura.

"Where are we?" She mumbled sleepily, sitting up. Her eyes widened in surprise when she stepped out of the car. "Is that the beach? Which beach?"

I chuckled. "Ventura. I rented us a beach house for the weekend. I thought, this far away from the city, we can explore the shops, hang out on the beach, do actual things outside of the apartments."

Fiona squealed with glee and jumped on me. I laughed and held her. "I take it this is a good surprise, then?"

"The best!" She kissed me quickly, then rushed to take off her shoes. "I love the feel of the sand in my toes." The only time I had ever seen her this giddy, was when she was playing with her computer.

She may or may not have messed with Keith a few times, payback for watching us that one night. Gay porn just kept finding its way onto his computer. She refused to admit to anything though, plausible deniability for me.

"Please tell me you packed me a bathing suit." She sighed with her eyes closed for a short moment, sinking her toes into the sand as far as she could.

"And if I didn't, what then?"

Her eyes sparkled like the moonlight on the ocean. "Then you better hope this is a private beach because I am sunbathing one way or the other." She cut off in a yelp when I roughly pulled her to me with one arm and laid one on her.

"I'm starting to wish I had left your bathing suit at home."

"Just because I wear it down there doesn't mean it will stay on. How public is this beach?"

"Zero. It's private. Belongs to one of my clients."

"Perfect." Fiona stepped back from me and pulled the blouse over her head, not worrying about the buttons this time. I watched as the pants landed on top of them in the sand. "Catch me if you can."

I waited in a frozen state for about five seconds, as her beautiful body ran toward the ocean. My clothes were gone seconds later.

She was already in the water, dipping her long hair in by the time I caught up to her. I didn't give her a chance to speak, or to tease me like I knew she would. I just kissed her and lifted her out of the water. Fiona kindly wrapped her wet arms and legs around me.

I was done waiting. I barely made it to the shoreline before laying her down in the wet sand to possess her. Waves of pleasure ran through us as the waves of the ocean coated our bodies.

I looked down on her beautiful face, pushing the wet hair behind her ear. "How did I get so lucky to have you in my life? What did I do that was worthy of your affection?"

Even with only the moonlight, I could see her blush heating her cheeks.

"I love you." Well, that just slipped out of me.

I had never even thought about those 3 little words before. Yikes. I guess this was a decently romantic setting, if I ever was going to say it, I could never beat a moonlit private beach for our first time.

"I love you, too." She whispered, almost in awe. Did she just realize it like I did?

I kissed her with reverence, still in a bit of shock over what we just said. Even what came next held a different tone than we'd ever had before.

After laying together for a little longer, watching the stars, feeling the ocean waves around us, and holding the most perfect angel in my arms, we decided to go clean up. The house was close enough that we weren't even close to dry when we reached it.

The shower took a while - since I insisted on searching her for every grain of sand.

My client was kind enough to have his personal chef leave a few pre-cooked meals for us. While I unpacked, Fiona warmed up a batch of enchiladas for us, wearing nothing but one of my shirts. I was only wearing briefs, so it was a good fit. It was my preferred way for her to cook. The fact that my briefs never succeeded in hiding just how much I enjoyed the show made her happy. It was a win-win situation.

The next day, we explored the little tourist stores nearby. We ate lunch at a small restaurant on the beach. We walked along the boardwalk, holding hands, kissing on occasion, full out making out behind a set of public bathrooms and changing rooms. The perfect day.

And it had the perfect end, a repeat of the night before.

Sunday, we spent the day sunbathing, just as Fiona requested. Without the bathing suits, just as I requested. I practically begged for a picture as I held her against my chest. At first, I thought it was because it was proof we were together. But no. It was because we weren't exactly covered. I promised to be careful. I teased her a few times with not being zoomed in enough, but I did eventually get one of us.

I thought I would have to make a deal with her to get her to take a picture of both of us, zoomed out. With my hands acting as the bikini top. Surprisingly, she agreed.

I failed to tell her when her finger slipped and hit the record button on my phone. By then, her eyes were closed, and the phone was tipping. I watched on the screen as my fingers worked her. When the phone tipped further down, I slid my fingers with it. She got a great shot of them sinking in and pumping. I double-checked later, and it recorded her sounds perfectly, as well. I now had a favorite video, and many favorite pictures that I cut from it.

Fiona had a contented smile on her face as we drove home that night. I took her straight up to her apartment and put her to bed. We didn't sleep for hours, but we did eventually fall asleep.

As she was fading out, she mumbled, "thank you for the perfect weekend away, Dillan. I love you so much."

I kissed the side of her head, finally putting a name to the feeling she always gave me. Love. Being with Fiona, thinking about Fiona, it filled me with love.

"I love you too, princess."

She sighed contentedly and fell asleep in my arms.

"Earth to Dillan!!"

I blinked my eyes a few times and slapped the hand away that was flying around in front of my face. "Knock it off."

"Oh, good, you haven't completely checked out." Jorge sighed, like that had been a legit concern.

"Anything new?"

"Yes. Now that we are closer, I can get a better lock on the computer she is using."

"She's still on?"

"Yes and no. She has a program running, but she already has access to what she needs. My best guess, she is buying time for us to catch up to her."

"What are you doing then?" The way his fingers were still moving, he was up to something.

"I am making use of a backdoor she opened for me into their database. And we aren't talking the hotel database, we are talking Russian mafia database. They ticked off the wrong girl today."

I snorted with only partial amusement. "They thought they did their homework but didn't look deep enough."

"Only thing I've never understood about Fiona is why she didn't go rogue. She has the skills."

I shook my head. "Fiona has the skills, and a little bit of the darkness in her. I think on some level, she works for the good side because she is afraid of what she could become if she didn't. When she lets her guard down, there is more darkness hiding in there. She hides it well. She has always been the one to help people. To take care of them. Over time, she expanded that to include what she loves to do."

"Yeah, I guess that makes sense. Anyhoo, I'm collecting all the stuff I can on the Russians, anything that can be used against them. With Fiona's help I've already been able to send proof to the Italians about Ivan's plan. He's got someone on the inside there as well. This wasn't a whim of his."

"And the rest?"

"Saving it for a rainy day. In case you need it later. Her idea. She sent a pic of rain."

Chapter 15

Fiona

"Aren't you done yet?" The guard snarled from his corner.

"Not quite. I'm not just hacking into someone's bank account and wiring money. I have to leave careful trails, change the dates of withdrawals and deposits. It all takes time to make sure it is done right. The last thing any of us need is to have Dillan and the Italians figure it all out. Frankly, I'm tempted to take a little for myself and start over somewhere far away from here."

He chuckled. "I bet Ivan would make a deal with you. Reserve your work for just us, and he will *give* you that money. You can live anywhere in the world that you want. We'd keep an eye on your brother and father, and you could finally be free."

Before a couple of months ago, that would have been very tempting. Too bad for them, I had someone I could no longer leave behind. Someone who was now part of my heart. My soul. Which was how I knew he was getting close. Jorge couldn't tell me anything without us getting caught. He tried, and I taught him a lesson. But the fact that he was picking up every crumb I could leave behind was answer enough.

"Guess we will have to see what happens after this, won't we?"

"True." My new chatty friend said. "If you betray us, or the plan fails, then you won't have much freedom or use - not on the computer anyway."

"I doubt I would be much use the other way either. I'm a geek through and through. Not much goes on in my life in the real world."

He sat up straight. "Does that mean you are a virgin? Please tell me you are a virgin."

I feigned confusion. "Uh, yeah. Why? What does that matter?"

His eyes sparked hungrily. "I love me a virgin. Nice, tight…"

"Neil, keep in your pants." Ivan said from the door. "If anyone gets take virginity, is me."

Ew. I'd rather have Neil. At least he wasn't nearly my father's age. "That won't be an issue though because this is going to work just fine. My plans always do."

"Then we have hope your plan no betray us."

I shrugged like none of this mattered to me in the least bit. "I don't really have a reason to betray you. Dillan's a butt wipe. He deserves what he gets. My brother has been warned to stop gambling, but he didn't, so he pretty much deserved it as well. I don't know the Italians, and I don't really care to. You all wanna kill each other, that's your choice. I just want to live my life."

Ivan grunted, possibly with a little respect. I wasn't sure though. "Why you work in such confining place? Your spirit shout be free."

"Steady money. Great benefits. Job security. What more could a girl want?"

"Freedom make own rules, own hours, and more money. I saw your face in conference room. You enjoy rush of hacking."

"I won't deny that fact. Right now, I can do it without getting in trouble. My bosses literally sit there and watch me. No one knows exactly what I am doing, they just assume I am proving a point."

Both men laughed, catching the hidden meaning.

"How much have you taken?" Neil asked, still laughing.

"None yet. I was just promoted to Junior Partner. I want to make sure that I am secure in my position and their trust in me. I also need the clients to trust me. That way, *if* they were to discover something, no one would look at sweet, little, old me."

"You smart little girl. But we see what happen. How much longer?" Ivan leaned against the doorframe, relaxed, without a care in the world. Like I posed no threat.

Little did they know…

"I should be done anytime now. Just a few more transactions, and it will look like this has been going on for a year. I decided to use two people from Dillan's side. It made more sense that way. His techie, who is supposed to be good at his job, already failed once when I broke in. It won't be hard to assume that he failed on purpose, maybe even took advantage of the situation. And then there is Keith, Dillan's right-hand man, and a creep. He is the money man. He tracks all of the money coming in and out. This way, when Dillan finds out, he won't question how he missed so many transactions for so long. Then there are the Italians. A little trickier since I don't know any of them. I made their side more generalized. That way they keep guessing. I have a program routing the money through various banks before it gets to yours, so they can't ever track it."

Neil whistled. "No wonder it's taken you so long."

I winked at him. "For anyone else, this would have taken a couple days. Like I said, my talents lie in computers." He licked his lips hungrily at the reminder. I would let BoBo handle him. "Stop looking at me like that. I can find all of your secrets on here too. I can multitask."

He hmphed defensively. "I ain't got no secrets." He then dramatically rubbed himself through his pants.

I snorted out a laugh. "Everyone has secrets. It's only a matter of knowing where to look to find them."

I quickly hacked into his phone from where I sat and found a certain type of video. I didn't know who the woman was, but it was obvious she was on the younger side. She also looked a little scared. And considering the force he used, I doubted he cared that she was so scared. Possibly not even willing. That was okay though, he was sure to be dead soon anyway. I saved a copy for myself, so I could find her and tell her the good news.

Neil's phone dinged with a message a moment later. He pulled it out, then dropped his phone on the floor. He frantically tried to pick it up before anyone else saw it.

"You don't mess with me, and I won't mess with you."

Ivan laughed. "What was secret?"

I shrugged but didn't answer. He laughed harder and turned to Neil.

"I may have recorded my date the other night without her permission. That's all." He turned to me with a scowl. "Point taken. And know, the minute I get the all clear, I will teach you a thing or two about respect."

"And you should know, if I can get that so easily, imagine what else I can get." I winked at him.

Women always knew when they were being recorded. We just often let the men think otherwise because they enjoyed thinking they were being naughty.

The room was silent while I continued roaming through everything with a fine-tooth comb. A small timer appeared in the corner of the screen, the one I had blocked from their view. Someone else liked thinking he was being naughty. At least he finally figured out how to keep it a secret.

Curious, I pulled up the street cameras. I noticed half a dozen black SUVs coming in fast.

I shifted over to the security cameras for the warehouse and looped them. I accessed the alarms around the main gate and shut them off. No one would know my rescuers were here. Not until they broke down the door. I then closed out of all the tabs but the ones they knew I was on. I didn't bother wiping the history, there was no point.

By the time the program finished running, it wasn't Dillan and the Italian's money that would be missing.

Ivan walked over to me, squatting down to get a better look at the computer. I tilted my head up to look at him defiantly.

"What's the matter? Don't trust me?"

I kept myself from flinching as he dragged a knuckle around my jaw and down my neck. "No even close." He hummed as his hand went lower. "How much longer until program done?"

"Half an hour, hour tops."

"And you need do anything else, or is independent now?"

"Why?"

Ivan slid his hand down the front of my shirt. "Because I am hungry and bored. And you only meal here." He went inside my bra and felt out every inch of me. "Such enticing meal too. You look sweet, but you have much spice in you. I bet, once we wake up beast, you be real player. What you say, little hacker? Let me teach you new tricks?"

I stared him down, daring him to push me. "No, thank you. I'm good."

He hummed. "Oh… but be bad can be much fun." He taunted, pinching me in a very delicate spot.

I hissed. I was a bit sore from Dillan. I always was really.

Ivan gave me a curious look, then began to roughly unbutton my shirt. It was a dark enough shade that I didn't need an undershirt. I hardly wore them anymore unless the top shirt required it. The undershirts just got in the way when Dillan was around.

I wanted to turn my head, admit my guilt, my lie, but I didn't. I kept my gaze steadily on the cretin in front of me as he saw the marks Dillan left the night before. He had kissed them in the shower this morning, telling each of them he loved them. Which made me laugh, until he went lower and told something else that he loved it.

Once that lid had come off, he was all for saying those three little words at any opportune moment.

"Virgin, huh?" Ivan grunted.

"I said I was a virgin, not completely innocent. There are a lot of things you can do in the meantime."

He chuckled. "This true. But that be best part. You missing out."

I shrugged. "We each have our own interests."

Ivan started circling what he could see of the marks. "These look done by someone who know what they doing."

"It certainly felt like he did."

"These no done by the man you kiss goodbye at office."

It was my turn to look confused. It took a minute or two to figure out who he was talking about.

"Oh. Chris has never touched me beyond kissing my cheek. No, he didn't leave them."

"You act like he was boyfriend."

I winked. "Girls gotta keep her options open. Haven't you ever thought about having fun behind an unlocked door?"

"No. I no think about things I want. I *take* what I want." He gripped me tight enough to make me yell out. "And I want… taste. You did what I said, my men take from here."

Randy moaned from the floor, finally showing signs of life.

Ivan grinned as he reached around to unclasp my bra. "I think demonstration front of brother ought to help him see error of ways."

I couldn't help it… I smacked the creep's hands away. Ivan growled and grabbed my hair, pulling me to my feet. I kicked out at him. He slapped me across the face hard enough to make me fall back to the floor. He squatted down again, hovering over me.

"You need to learn place, little hacker."

I wiped my arm off dramatically, with a look of disgust. "And you need to learn to say it, not spray it."

That earned me another backhanded slap. He pushed me onto my back and tried to pin me. I made two fists and started hitting him. Neil jumped in then and grabbed both of my arms, pinning them under his legs.

Ivan was just unbuckling my pants when we heard a dozen pairs of feet running down the hall.

"Sir!" The lead man shouted, not even blinking an eye at our position. "The Italians here, armed teeth. What you want us do?"

Gees, his take on the English language was almost worse than Ivan's.

Ivan growled and ripped my pants open. "You betray us! Who you contact? How?" His pause was slight as it came to him. "They watch screen?"

"Sir!" The man called him again, right as the gunfire started.

Ivan growled. "Kill them all."

"Yes, sir." The man ran back out, leaving me with two angry men and one out-cold brother.

"Tell me what you do, little hacker. Who you contact?"

"Someone you never should have gone against." I told him haughtily. "He's going to kill you when he gets here. You really should have done your homework better, or maybe found someone better to spy for you."

Ivan snarled at me as he lifted his hand to hit me again.

"I suggest you stop and rethink what you are about to do, Ivan." The command was relaxed but forceful. And emphasized with the sound of a gun being cocked.

I closed my eyes and sighed. I knew he would come.

"Dillan." Ivan said calmly. "This no concern you. None this does." He lowered his hand from where it definitely had been preparing to strike me again, but he still had me pinned, half-naked, under him. And right under the piece that said he was enjoying our positioning more than I was.

"Oh, it concerns me very much. And not just because you were trying to force me into a war with the Italians."

Ivan's hand came out of nowhere as it smacked across my cheek again, with an angry growl. He was off me seconds later, lying on the ground, the side of his head bleeding around the fingers holding it.

Neil was already dead at BoBo's feet, his head twisted at an odd angle. Dillan moved to kneel next to me, his hands hovering around helplessly. Gone was the calm scary demeanor, now was the concerned boyfriend.

"Are you alright? How late am I?"

I started to sit up, and he moved in to help me. "Just in time actually. He only hit me a few times, that's it."

"Why hell you help her? She hack computers. She lock you out!" Ivan growled from the floor, trying to stand back up, using the wall to maintain his balance. It looked like it had been a hard hit. I was sure he was dizzy.

Dillan helped me stand, and then carefully buttoned my shirt before holding me.

"She did, but then we talked things over and made peace." He grazed a gentle hand around the bruises threatening to form on my face. "Now, she is the love of my life." Dillan turned back to look at Ivan, leaning against the wall. "And you tried to take her from me." His gun raised again.

But someone else shot first and Ivan fell to the floor.

We all looked, shocked, at Randy, sitting against the other wall, holding a gun in the air. "It's my job to protect my sister, not the other way around. I think it's time I start doing that." His voice was barely understandable as he pushed out the words.

Right before grunting and falling back to the floor.

I ran over and checked his pulse again. I sighed. "He just passed back out."

Chapter 16

Ðillan

I almost didn't make it in time. It had taken longer to organize with Bruno than I thought it would. But then, I'd never had to organize a war party before.

Jorge sent the timer to Fiona, letting her know we were coming. He said she would know what to do from there. Considering we nearly got all the way to their front door before they knew we were here, when Bruno was expecting an earlier welcome, Jorge was right.

While Bruno and his men went in guns blazing, BoBo and I went in the direction Jorge had instructed us to go in before we left him with our car. The computer was off, but he had a good idea of where she was in the building. Being closer had helped him get better location specifics.

I didn't know if I would ever be able to get the image of Fiona being pinned down by two men twice her size out of my head.

I brought her back to my arms, where she was safe as soon as she was assured that Randy was still breathing.

"They probably broke a couple ribs this time. He had enough willpower to push through the pain to grab the gun Neil dropped, probably when he grabbed your arms. We will get him to a doctor as soon as it is safe to leave this room."

Fiona nodded once and leaned on me. "You're late."

I huffed and wrapped her in my arms. "I expected to find you curled in a ball and crying when I got here, not mouthing off to two men intent on hurting you."

Her laugh was shaky. "No, you didn't."

I squeezed her tighter, wishing I could always keep her safe right there. "No, I didn't. How are you, really?"

I lifted her chin up with my finger, so I could see in her eyes. The tears were beginning to form, her wall at the breaking point. She had really pushed herself mentally this time. I kissed each watery eye.

"I will get you home. I will keep you safe. Everyone knows you are mine now. No one will ever dare to hurt you again. If I have to build an army to stand guard around you, I will. According to Jorge, I now have the money for it."

Her tears slid out then, her small smile wobbling. "I was scared spitless, Dillan."

"I know, princess. The more scared you are, the mouthier you get."

"Wait. Does that mean you *were* scared of me when you came to the club?" BoBo broke in.

"Out of my freaking mind." Fiona mumbled into my shirt. "I'd never faced one of my brother's bookies before. Hell, I'd never been to a club before."

BoBo cursed with a laugh. "I thought I was either losing my touch, or you were just that crazy. I've been leaning more towards the latter."

Fiona flipped him off.

We waited a few minutes longer, until the warehouse grew silent. Bruno came through after that.

"Time to go. The clean-up crew are ready to start."

"Did you get everyone?"

"Everyone here, yes. But they only had a small force here. Enough to set them back for a bit, especially while they scramble to crown a new pakhan. The cops won't be held back much longer. We need to go." His eyes raked over the room. "Any of them coming with us?"

"Yes, my brother." Fiona pointed at him.

Bruno nodded once, then waved for someone to grab him. He then turned back to Fiona, offering her his hand.

"Bruno Gallo, nice to meet you. You are one smart cookie, ma'am."

Fiona didn't say anything, just buried herself more into me. She was going to need some time before she was ready to face people. She didn't care much for socializing before, I suspected it would be non-existent for a while. Bruno didn't seem to mind, he gave her a soft smile, which changed rapidly when he caught the state of her pants.

"I stopped them just in time." I answered his unasked question, but the anger was still brimming. I was a little ticked that Randy stole my thunder. Given, he probably needed it more than I did.

I *really* wanted to be the one to kill that guy, though.

"Good." Bruno kicked Neil's side. "Guys like this give both Russians and mafia a bad name. I know a few Russians, like them just fine even. But these guys…" He huffed. Then cursed in Italian and spit on them.

He left without another word. I lifted Fiona up into my arms, not bothering to ask her first, and carried her out. BoBo followed right behind us.

We loaded into the SUVs, Fiona still on my lap, safely tucked in my arms. We waited a few more minutes, then three men came running out, laughing. A minute later, an orange glow illuminated the insides. As we pulled away, the flames began to eat the exterior of the building.

"How is that cleaning up?" Fiona asked softly.

"They covered all the bodies with gasoline and circled the building. By the time the fire department gets out here, all the evidence of our presence will be gone." Bruno explained calmly from the front seat.

"Oh, that makes sense." We all chuckled softly at her blase attitude.

The car stopped half an hour later, letting us out where we left our own car. I expected to see Jorge waiting anxiously, exactly the way we left him when I insisted he stay behind. But he wasn't there.

Someone else was.

"Hey. Everything alright?" I stepped out of the car awkwardly, still holding the clinging woman in my arms.

The longer she had to dwell on what happened, the tighter she held onto me. I needed to get her home. Where she felt safe enough to let it all out.

Keith stepped forward, like he might offer to help, but stopped when Fiona's grip on my shirt visibly tightened.

"You tell me." He answered, looking at her. They'd only met a few times, but each time she had been completely different than this.

"Yeah. Everything is good. The villain is dead, and the damsel rescued."

BoBo snorted. "Damsel." He repeated it like it was a joke.

He got another middle finger from my girl. Which made me feel a little better.

Bruno rolled his window down behind me and I turned to look at him. "I will take the brother to the hospital for you, we shouldn't keep moving him. I will tell them I found him on the side of the street like that. His best bet would be to say he was mugged."

"Thank you. I'd shake your hand, but…"

His grin didn't quite reach his eyes. "But someone else needs them more. We are even now, yes?"

"Yes, we are. Until the next time a pretty cop gets close to you."

He laughed as they pulled away.

Keith opened the car door for me, while BoBo went to the front seat. Minutes later, we pulled away and headed home.

"What happened to Jorge?"

"I sent him home in my car. He didn't go easily. You know he's been dying to meet Fiona, and he wanted to make sure she was okay. I convinced him this wasn't the best time."

I nodded. "Did you know he was gay?" That was still bugging me.

Keith's shock was enough of an answer. "No way." His denial was more of a whisper.

"Yeah. He made a comment about wanting to kiss Fiona. He bailed himself out of trouble by telling me about his boyfriend. I just have no clue who it is."

"Your bartender. The dorky one." Fiona yawned, resting her head under my neck.

"Kent?"

Fiona giggled softly at how we all asked together. "Sure. It's all over Jorge's social media."

"Since when do you follow him?" This woman never stopped surprising me.

"I don't. I hacked his account. It's a game we've been playing. He keeps trying to one-up me. Really, I just keep getting more points."

"No wonder he is half in love with you."

She tipped her chin up enough to kiss my neck. "Too bad I love someone else."

Feeling that rush of love again, I looked down into her eyes. It wasn't long before I kissed her softly. I was vaguely aware of Keith crawling up to the front seat, grumbling. It wasn't like I was going to do anything to her. Not right now. Not when the memories of those men on top of her were still fresh in her mind.

Still, I let her rotate enough to sit on my lap. And I took great pleasure in kissing her long and hard, reminding myself she was back where she belonged.

What felt like minutes later, BoBo pulled up to her apartment.

"I thought we were going back to your place." She mumbled as I kissed down her neck.

"And I thought you might prefer to be in your own place tonight. Somewhere more familiar and comfortable."

"Thank you. But either place would have been fine. I am perfectly comfortable at your place."

I hummed. I liked the sound of that.

"Will you two just get out of this car already?" Keith half whined, half commanded.

"Yeah, yeah, yeah." I climbed out first, then waited for Fiona to join me. I lifted her again since her pants still showed a little too much.

"What's wrong? What happened?" The security guard, whose name I really should have gotten by now, came running over.

"She's okay. Just had a really bad day."

"Do I need to call in the night shift early?"

"No. The threat has been eliminated. She will be safe now. Thank you, though."

Fiona laid in my arms quietly as I carried her through the lobby and up the elevator. I carried her all the way into her bathroom, having stopped long enough for her to lock the front door behind us.

"We should really just consolidate our apartments. This going back and forth thing is getting old."

I carefully removed her clothes, keeping an eye out for more bruises. "Is that your way of asking me to officially move in?" I smiled up at her from where I was pulling her pants off her feet. I closed my eyes, enjoying the feeling of her hands in my hair.

"Well, it's not like you asked me to move in with you."

I stood up, lifting her onto the counter, and pressed my forehead to hers. "I don't care where we live, as long as I have you. As long as I can fall asleep with you in my arms and wake up to your hair in my face." I slid my fingers through her hair but stopped to grab the back of her head. "I love you, Fiona Reynolds.

A tear slid down her face and wiped it with my thumb.

"I love you too, Rolland Dillan Murphy."

I groaned. "I'm not even going to ask how you found that name. Please never say it again. You have no idea how many times I was teased for it as a kid."

She giggled and wrapped her arms around my neck. "I like it. Rolland." It almost sounded better coming from her. Almost.

"You can call me that if you want." She grinned greedily. "But then I will be calling you Pixie."

That grin quickly turned into a frown. "You wouldn't dare."

"Oh, wouldn't I? I feel like you should know me better than that by now."

"Gah, fine."

I saw the tick of her lips and jumped in to cut off the next one. "No Dill Pill either."

Fiona stuck her tongue out at me. I quickly caught it with my teeth. She quickly forgot what we were talking about.

What were we talking about?

I was perfectly happy just kissing my naked girlfriend, the love of my life, but the naughty little thing started in on my pants. I panted as I pulled away from her.

"We don't have to. Not until you're ready."

"Dillan, shut up and get in here."

"Yes, ma'am." I saluted her as she pushed the constrictive material down.

I held her against me sometime later, grateful I hadn't turned the shower on yet, not quite ready to leave her body. When I moved my head back, she came off my chest and looked up at me.

"You scared the hell out of me today. Katia came running to the club, completely frantic. Don't worry, I had Jorge send her and Linda a message. You can call them later." The new tension in her shoulders began to relax again. "I didn't know what to do. I ran into your office like a complete lunatic. Shouting for Linda because I didn't know which office was yours. I had a Senior Partner monitoring me to make sure I wasn't a danger. I nearly lost it when I saw your note. When Gary told me who you had gone to lunch with… I…" I trailed off, all my fear finally breaking through the surface.

I just got her, and I already nearly lost her. I wasn't sure I would ever come back from something like that.

Scratch that. I knew I wouldn't. I knew now that I had barely been living before Fiona stomped into my life. If she were to leave me now, I would be worse off than I had ever been before.

"Sh… sh… sh, I'm here now. You followed the breadcrumbs. You didn't hesitate or doubt me. You found me and saved me, Dillan. You took care of me, you always do."

"Fi…" My voice cracked again, and I was pretty sure that was a tear rolling down my cheek. "I barely kept it together. Chris got far enough into your computer that we knew about Randy. Jorge showed up and took over from there. I was doing good. But when I saw the picture…"

Fiona scrunched her eyes, not sure what I was talking about.

"Us on the beach. You kept saying you had to keep us a secret, but then you went and put a picture of us up in your office."

"I figured it didn't matter if they knew I had a boyfriend, just who it was. And seeing you there with me every day made it that much better. Like I wasn't living two separate lives." She tried to act like it was no big deal, but I knew her better than that.

"It was nearly my undoing again. I know you say you love me, but something about you having a piece of me in your professional life… it really affected me, Fi. It made me need to find you even more. I didn't think it was possible to love you more than I already did, but I do."

"I knew you were coming. I kept telling myself that you were coming. At the same time, I had to make Ivan think I hated you and that was why I hacked your system in the first place. I had to make him believe it. Then I heard your voice, and I felt it deep in my bones. The word had just come that you were there. The attack just started, and you were already there to save me. You didn't waste any time finding me today, Dillan. I get what you are saying. Knowing, seeing you put me above all else, above your own safety. You called in mafia ties you don't want, all to save me. Hearing your voice, feeling your arms around me, gave me the peace I needed. My love for you grows more and more every day. I need you more than I have ever needed anyone."

It was a long time before we made it to that shower, but we did eventually make it.

While I warmed up something for dinner, Fiona made calls to Katia and Linda. Then she emailed Gary, from his own account, telling him she was taking the next couple of weeks off work. She said he would know for sure it was her that way.

We ate in our favorite fashion, with her on my lap, and me feeding her.

The next morning, I woke to her still in my arms, sleeping soundly. Usually she woke me up, as she had to get to work. It was always early enough that we could welcome the new day together. Not this morning though. This morning, my girl needed her sleep.

It hadn't been all that restful the night before. She had a few nightmares, more about them killing Randy or myself, than them hurting her. She woke up clinging to me tightly after those ones.

After a quick check through my missed messages, my people updating me, I slipped out and snuck into the bathroom, then slipped back into the bed. Her eyes were closed, but she cuddled into my side and draped her leg over me. I turned to my side, making sure I was in just the right spot on her and teased her. As soon as the whimpering started, I pushed her to her back and picked up where we left off the night before.

"With how often we do this, it's a good thing I have an IUD." Fiona laughed. "Not to mention how long you stay inside there."

I rocked into her again, making her moan. "It's my favorite place to be. Soft, warm, cozy. And all mine." I moved slowly, building us both back up. "Admit it, you don't want me to come out."

"Never."

Eventually, we climbed out of the bed in search of food.

"I need to go see Randy today." She told me, while feeding me a piece of bacon.

"No." She pulled the bacon back and glared at me. I tried to soften my voice. I didn't want to sound too overbearing. "You need to rest and lay low."

"I need to see my brother. I need to see that he is okay."

"BoBo sent a guard to watch over him. The pain meds are keeping him asleep for the most part. The cops and doctors all believe the story about the mugging. If you go, it's going to start new questions."

"Why? I'm his sister. His family."

"Yes, but you also look like you took a beating." I lightly grazed the bruises on her cheek. Fiona tried to hide the wince, but it didn't work. I saw through it. "You need to stay until you heal. And I need to keep you where you are safe. Where I can protect you."

Apparently, she saw through me too. She leaned back and held my head to her chest. I wouldn't complain about the position, just that my t-shirt covered too much of her.

"You can't keep me locked away forever."

I turned and bit her through the shirt. "Watch me." I ended up ripping the shirt off her so I could get a better bite.

Chapter 17

Fiona

I caved to Dillan and let him keep me locked up for nearly a week. If it hadn't been for the regular rotation of ice packs and ibuprofen, it would have been a great week. I needed to see Randy though.

With the help of a boatload of concealer and a face mask, most of the dark rainbow was covered.

Dillan dropped me off at the hospital, promising to be back as soon as I sent word. I forced him to go to the club, as he hadn't left my apartment in all that time either.

I found Randy lying in a hospital bed on the 3rd floor. I stood in the doorway and just stared at him. His guard sat near the window, but when he saw me, he stood up, nodded his head in greeting, and went out into the hall. Randy turned to look at me. He smiled, then frowned.

"It feels like just yesterday I was here with Dad. How are you feeling? Do you need a nursing home now too?"

"I probably should." His voice got a bit raspy with emotion, and he had to clear it before he could continue. "I have a problem. I didn't listen to you. I always thought you were overreacting with your warnings. I am so, so sorry, Fi." I'd never seen my brother cry. I'd seen him come close, but not actually cry like this.

I walked over and sat on the bed, holding him. He cried for a minute then pulled away, his eyes on the mask. When his hand went to move it, I stopped him.

"Don't. It won't help."

He nodded once and dropped his hand. "Did they… did… I could hear them talking. I was starting to come out of it. I got my eyes open enough to see you fall to the floor, and them… but then it went black again. I managed to open them again after I heard Dillan. I could see a gun close by and grabbed it. I couldn't let them hurt you. I can't stop seeing that man on top of you."

"They never got the chance. Dillan came before then. He's a little peeved you pulled the trigger first. He was really itching for it. But he also knows it was something you needed to do. You needed to feel the satisfaction of protecting me. He thinks that will help you heal faster, mentally. Not much we can do about the physical. How are you?"

"Concussion, a couple broken ribs, bruised pretty much everywhere inside. Had some internal bleeding. My leg will require surgery, but they wanted to get the rest of me stable first though. Does, uh, does Dad know?"

"No. I haven't figured out what to tell him yet. I don't want to stress out his heart. He's always known about the gambling though, Randy."

He snorted. "I kind of figured. He never came out and said it, but the way he would look at me with pity once in a while. I'm working on that though. A psych doctor with the hospital has come to talk to me a few times. She says addiction is a brain disease. But they can help me. We've been discussing possible triggers. Since it started when mom died, she is wondering if my trigger is the desire to take care of my family, but not having another way to do it. Instead, I went into a hole, and you dug me out. Then I felt guilty and wanted to pay you back. It was a never-ending circle. I told her that I owed people money and they had gone after you. I stepped in and got beat, but you got away. When she asked where you were, I told her you had gotten hit, but your boyfriend was taking care of you. I explained that he sent his little friend to stay with me as a consolation prize. They know I am not telling them the complete truth, but they are taking it for now. With therapy, the doc says I will get better. I really hope so."

His voice cracked as he looked at me again, his eyes focused on the mask. "I never want you to get hurt because of me again."

"I won't. Your future brother-in-law wouldn't allow it. You have no idea how much convincing it took for him to even let me leave the house today… What? What did I say?"

Randy's eyes were wide. "Did he propose? Already?"

I blushed, not that it would show through all the makeup. "No, not yet at least. I know he loves me. Even if he hadn't already said it, it would be obvious after the other day. We are talking about moving in together though. And from the way he rubs my stomach every time I talk to Katia, I'd say he is definitely thinking about the future."

"Wow. I never thought Dillan had it in him."

I shrugged. "Things change when you meet the right person. From the moment we first met, we just sort of clicked. Like everything was falling into place. I never gave much thought to soulmates and all of that girly crap, but now… I'm thinking it just might be true. He's everything I never thought to ask for."

Randy shook his head slowly. "I'm glad you found him then. It's a bit weird to think about you and him together. I never would have thought you would go for someone like him. I always pictured you with a nerdy computer geek kind of guy. I thought you would spend your nights at home messing with each other online."

"Oh no, I do that to his friends. Dillan sits right next to me, reading a book or watching a movie. His IT guy is a hoot. He is determined to beat me one day. I keep proving him wrong. Dillan says he is dying to meet me. We have never even messaged, just digital pranks."

"Why aren't you with him then?"

I laughed at the idiot. He really was struggling with the idea of me and his bookie. "For one, I was already falling for Dillan. And two, Jorge's gay."

"Ah. And no one at work…"

I elbowed the butthead. "There is a Junior Partner, my old boss, that I know likes me. He started coming around more, right about the time I met Dillan. At first, I thought if it hadn't been for Dillan, we might have been good together. But I'm starting to realize I never would have been happy with guys like that. I need someone who can take care of me once in a while. I need the Dark Knight. I need someone who gets it when I don't want to be the good girl all the time. I've always had to play that role in the family. I get a high when I hack into people's lives. I can do that at work and not get in trouble for it. I can even mess with Keith when he is being a butthead. Dillan thinks it's hilarious." I laid my head on my brother's shoulder. "I found where I belong with that crew. Even crabby BoBo."

Randy took my left hand in his and patted it. "I'm glad you found people who accept you, sis."

"You will find your place in the world, too, Randy. It will just take time."

"Maybe, but right now, I am more concerned with becoming a better brother and a better son."

He yawned, so I kissed his cheek and moved off the bed. "You already are, Randy. Get some rest. Love you."

His eyes were getting heavy, but he still smiled. "Love you too, Pixie."

"I'd hit you for that, but I'm not sure where I can do it without making you worse."

He grunted and closed his eyes. I stayed sitting nearby until he was completely out cold. When I finally left the room, I closed the door quietly behind me.

"How is he really?" I asked the guard sitting on a bench nearby.

"Doc says he will be fine. The surgery on his leg is scheduled for 3 days from now. The therapist comes in almost every day. He asks about you a lot. I'm sure this will help him relax some."

I blew out my breath. "Good. Thank you for staying with him. The big bully at home won't let me do much right now."

The guard laughed. "Yeah, I can see that. He was really freaked when that prego chick showed up telling him you were missing. I've never seen Dillan so off-kilter. It was very disconcerting. He'll calm down in time but will probably always be a little more overprotective than he was before."

I nodded. "Yep. Kind of figured that. Speaking of which, I should probably let him know I'm done. Randy fell back asleep a few minutes ago."

The guard lifted his phone and wiggled it. "He's been messaging me nonstop since you got here. I doubt he ever made it to the club. My bets are on him already being downstairs."

"Probably." I huffed. "Thanks. I'm Fiona, obviously." I raised my hand to him, and he took it.

"Eric. Nice to meet you. And welcome to the *Indecent* family."

I fought the laugh, then gave up. "That is definitely one way to describe this family of ours." With a small wave, and another thanks, I headed back out.

Sure enough, Dillan was standing outside the hospital doors, leaning against the town car.

"This is an emergency zone only, you know?" I stopped less than a foot in front of him, pulling the mask off my face so I could breathe again.

"It is an emergency."

"Really? And what is that?"

Dillan put a hand on my back and leaned into my ear. "It's been hours and hours since I got to be with you."

"You left me not even two hours ago, Dillan." I pressed against him, speaking softly in his ear. "You had me multiple times before that."

"It's not enough. It will never be enough." He gripped my waist and yanked me against him, while he nibbled on my neck.

"Not outside the hospital, Dillan."

"Whatever you say, princess."

He released me long enough to open the back door of the car. I was going to ask why, until he started lifting my baggy t-shirt. I jumped in with a squeak. He laughed as he followed me. I didn't even get a seatbelt on before his mouth was on mine.

When my brain came out of what I was now referring to as the "Dillan Fog," I was on the floor of the car, with no clothes.

"Has your car always been this big?"

Dillan laughed, kissing my forehead. "Yes, I just usually keep you on the seat. It's more comfortable."

That was about the time I realized that his wasn't the only laugh filling the space. I looked over his shoulder, squeaked, and tried to hide under him better. They both laughed harder.

"You both will pay for this."

"What did I do?" At least Dillan sounded a little concerned. Unlike someone else who was still laughing. "I didn't know he was here either. Honest."

"He didn't." Keith tried to stop his laughing long enough to defend his friend. "You two just really go into your own bubble. You are at the club, by the way. Since neither of you told BoBo where to go. You didn't answer my call, so I called him." His amusement died fast, and he cleared his throat awkwardly. "We have need of your assistance, Dillan."

Dillan started to turn toward him, but I screeched and pulled him back over. He was my only cover. He laughed and pet my head, trying to comfort me. It wasn't going to help until Keith was out of the car. And I had clothes on again.

"Bunny is screaming because no one will let her in the club."

"Didn't you tell her she was fired?" Dillan stopped himself from moving more than his head that time.

"Yes. But she obviously didn't believe me. I think she needs to hear it from you."

"Fine." Dillan sighed. "I'll be out in a minute."

I didn't hear the door after a minute, so I looked over again. Keith was still sitting there, playing on his phone.

"As in, get out, Keith." I lifted a foot and kicked him.

He tskd but opened the door. "You have 3 minutes to get dressed, or I'm coming back in and staying in." He slammed the door and leaned against the window. Thankfully. Now no one would see us.

Dillan looked down at my bare body and licked his lips. "I do love a good challenge.'

"Dillan…" I whimpered his name because he wasn't just licking himself now. "I don't want him to come back in."

"Why? It's not like either of us notice, so what difference does it make?"

At the moment, I had no clue. My brain had fogged again.

Until someone knocked on the window and yelled "2 minutes!"

"Dillan, please?"

He sighed and finally vacated my premises, throwing me his t-shirt. I didn't think about it, I just threw it on. "The things I do for you."

I snorted at the idiot and grabbed my leggings. "Where is my underwear?"

"No clue."

"1 minute!" Keith yelled again.

I squeaked and pulled my leggings up fast. Screw the underwear. Dillan laughed and pulled me onto his lap.

"I love you."

And that did it to me. I wasn't irritated with him anymore. The butthead.

I jumped when the door next to us suddenly opened.

"Darn, you're decent, well, mostly." Keith's eyes traveled down to where my hand was.

I noticed Dillan's head fall back with his eyes closed. Seeing as it wasn't me that was exposed, I figured why not. And I was curious what Keith would do. So, I kept pumping Dillan. When he grabbed my head, I obliged and went down to my knees. Once again, I forgot about Keith.

I kissed my way up the bare chest as I climbed back on Dillan's lap, then snuggled into him. He hugged me tight before moving me to the seat.

"I need to deal with this, then I will be back. Stay here."

I curled up on my side and closed my eyes. I didn't care about their little problem. I'd had enough drama lately to last a lifetime anyway.

Chapter 18

Dillan

"Where is the varmint?" I stepped out of the car while zipping up my pants.

"Over near the backdoor. She's been bouncing between trying to get into the studio and trying to get into the club. Don't you wanna put a shirt on first?"

We slowly started making our way around the building. "I'll probably regret it, but no. I gave it to Fiona. She hasn't realized it yet, but I literally tore her shirt off her back at the hospital."

Keith scratched his jaw, trying to hide the smile of what he no doubt had seen in that car. He had more kinks in him than I did. "Is it just me, or are you two worse now than you were before?"

"We are. Mostly because every time I see the bruises on her face, I start freaking out again. I came so close to losing her, to her losing herself. That scene… it won't leave me, Keith. I can't…" I stopped walking and took a deep breath. "Being away from her today, for the first time since it happened, was too much. I couldn't get the different scenarios out of my head. I worry the rest of the Bratva will come at her for revenge."

"The Italians kept you guys out of it. And everyone involved was inside that building."

"I know that. I do. But I still can't stop worrying. She wants to go back to work as soon as the bruises fade, I don't know if I can let her go that long."

"You both have to keep living your lives. You can't put them on hold. And if you try to hold her back, she will start to resent you for it. Besides, you know where she works now. You can take her to lunch or pick her up from work."

"If she still has a job. She's worried about what they will say now. If this had all been tied to them, that would be different. But it wasn't. It was all due to Randy."

"Hello, lover. It's been so long."

I cringed at the cold hands suddenly running up and down my bare chest. Behind me, Bunny rubbed her cheek on my back.

Before I could say a word, her hands were gone, and she was screeching.

"Back the hell off, skank. You've been warned time and time again. You spied, you shared information you shouldn't have, and you nearly got us all killed. Get gone before I make you join your little boyfriend permanently."

"Holy hell, that was hot." Keith whispered.

I nodded silently, watching my girl scowl down at the little runt. Bunny's eyes jumped between Fiona and me, settling on my shirt that she was wearing. It was one of my favorites, one Bunny no doubt recognized.

"Baby?" She looked at me pleading, like she was honestly confused at what was going on.

I moved behind Fiona, wrapping an arm around her, and kissing her neck softly. "I told you to stay in the car."

"You took too long, and then I saw her walking up behind you. You know how I feel about others touching you."

I hummed and nibbled. "I do. I would do the same." My eyes lifted to Bunny's incredulous expression. "You know the rules, Bunny. You keep breaking them. You've already been fired and warned. Come back again, and you will pay the permanent consequences."

I took Fiona's hand and dragged her around the pile of trash, not wanting her to dirty herself any more than she already had. "Take out the trash, Keith."

"Yes, sir. Let's go… come on… That's it..." His voice died away as I pulled Fiona around to the back of the building.

I immediately pressed her against the wall. "That was the hottest thing I have ever seen."

She giggled. "It felt really good. Protecting what's mine."

I kissed her roughly, then forced myself off her. I began pulling her again. "Not in a dirty alley. You are better than that." I pulled her through the back door, and into the elevator.

Fiona stopped my hand before it could reach the screen to call the elevator. With an evil little smile, she put her own thumb on the pad and called it. I growled out a laugh and pulled her back to me.

"Forget to tell me something, princess?"

"No. I gave you back your access. I just didn't take mine all the way out. You didn't specify that I had to."

We didn't make it all the way up to the studio. Not at first.

We stayed there the rest of the day, so I could work and still have her nearby. Not that I left the studio to do any of that.

Fiona was asleep in the bed when Keith came in that evening.

"We've got a problem." He kept his voice low, not wanting to wake her.

"What's wrong?" I matched his level as I moved further away from her and closer to where he stood at the door.

"Russians are here. They just came in. They are looking around, probably for you."

I hustled over to the dresser and pulled out a fresh pair of jeans and a black shirt. "Who is leading them? Do we know?"

"It looks like Ivan's younger brother. Without an heir, the Bratva would look to him for leadership."

I picked up my shoes and carried them out the door as we left. "What's our relationship with him like?"

Keith shrugged, kicking the bra still on the elevator floor out into the walkway before the studio. "Don't really have one. He wasn't local until recently. Your guess is as good as mine."

By the time we stepped off in front of the office, I was put together and ready to work.

"Go down and bring him up. We're going to need privacy for this." I sat behind my desk and opened the computer like I was going to be working, business as usual.

Keith smirked and walked back out.

Feeling curious, I logged into my database and looked through all of my employees and everyone who was cleared to use the elevator. I couldn't find her.

I blinked rapidly, startled, when the screen suddenly changed on me. I was looking at my database, but a different side of it. I saw her name listed, but it wasn't Fiona. The person listed as the main administrator was Princess Fiona - Ruler of All Things Indecent.

I laughed. Hard.

I laughed even harder when a picture of Princess Fiona from *Shrek* filled the screen. It was the one of her looking out the window of the castle she was locked in, looking sad and depressed. Then a clip of Shrek battling his way through the castle appeared. Then of him walking away after letting the evil guy take his princess. I picked up my phone and messaged her.

Me: I did not abandon you. There is an issue I need to deal with. And Keith is not the villain.
MyPrincess: I call it like I see it. *sad face emoji*

I sighed. This woman could really get to me. I couldn't help laughing though when my computer screen showed Princess Fiona pulling apart the flower, saying "he loves me, he loves me not, he loves me, he loves me not."

Me: You doubt?
Me: If there is one thing in this world you should never doubt, it's how much I love you. I will be back up soon. I promise. Get some sleep because I plan on keeping you up the rest of the night.

My office door opened, and Keith held it for three men to enter. I leaned back in my chair as I watched them. One sat down, the other two stood behind him.

"Welcome to my club. I don't believe we've had the pleasure of meeting before. My name is Dillan, and I own everything in this domain."

"My name is Viktor Smirnov. I believe you knew my brother. And had hand in killing him." The fists behind him clenched. His accent was thick, but he seemed to have a better handle on the language than Ivan had.

"I won't deny that because there'd be no point. Did I pull the trigger? No. But I was ready to, and would have, had someone else not beat me to it."

Viktor's eyes creased in a way that showed he was trying to hold in his anger. "You so carelessly talk about murdering my only brother, our pakhan?"

I snorted. "Carelessly? No. Just thinking about it makes me want to raise him from the dead just to kill him myself. We had a peace pact between us. We all stayed in our own little corners. The Italians, the Russians, and me. Both families often came to my establishment. Your brother even used my fighting ring from time to time. Ask the man behind you, he was a frequent fighter. Everything was fine until your brother decided to cross the line. He kidnapped my girlfriend and held her hostage. She is a cyber genius. He forced her to hack into my bank accounts and that of the Italians. He was trying to corner me into a war I was ill-equipped to handle. He thought I would run to him for help. So many times, I have turned down his offer of partnership. He got tired of being turned down. My girl is smart, she managed to feed me information without him knowing. I found her right as he was about to violate her in the worst way possible. She still has bruises across her face from him. So, no, gentlemen, I have no reason to feel guilty about killing him or to hide it. On the contrary. I want everyone to know that if they mess with the people I love, they will pay for it."

The screen on the computer changed to a flower with the last petal falling off, with the caption "he loves me" under it.

I groaned and rubbed my eyes. Keith lifted an eyebrow at me, I pointed at the screen while looking in the direction of the camera in my ceiling.

"Woman, go to bed and stop spying on me." I turned back to the confused faces of the three men. "I should have known better than to fall for a hacker. The night we met; she locked me out of my whole system. Now…" I saw a video of Fred Flintstone banging on the front door, yelling for his wife, playing on my screen. With a sigh I turned my laptop around for them to see. "She's doing this from her cell phone."

The men snickered and I turned it back around in time to see the screen flash and go blank. I shook my head, deciding I probably didn't want to know.

"Look, I'm sorry you lost your brother. Ivan and I were doing fine until he took her. We can have the same deal again, but if you choose to escalate this, I will understand."

Viktor looked uncomfortable as he glanced at the back of the computer, making my curiosity spike again.

I glanced at the screen when the color change drew my attention. This time it was a black-and-white shot from the old show *Hogan's Heroes*, where the bigger soldier was saying "I know nothing, nothing!"

That woman. Keith stood behind me, watching it as well. Trying not to laugh.

"What's it going to be, Viktor?"

He cleared his throat and stood up. "You keep to your side, and we will keep to ours. Any chance you will give me the name of the person who killed him? We already know the Italians were involved." His eyes drifted back to my computer, "now we know why the video footage was looping the entire time until the signal crashed from the fire."

I stood up with them, now ignoring the meme on the screen with the baby sister from *Despicable Me*, the words saying "Not lil ole innocent me."

Someone needed a spanking tonight.

"No, I won't. They were trying to protect her, so they have earned my protection as well."

He nodded like he expected me to say that. "I can't guarantee that some of our men won't cause any problems, they want revenge for the death of the pakhan. I will also keep searching for who killed my brother."

"I appreciate the warning. We will be ready and waiting."

He nodded again and walked toward the stairs, Keith following behind.

I dropped onto the small couch and put my head in my hands. When I heard the ding of the elevator opening, I quietly waited for Keith to come in. What I got instead were smaller hands pushing me to lean back on the couch. Then one slender leg moved to either side of me. My eyes trailed up from the boy shorts she was wearing to the sports bra.

"You were playing with fire tonight." I told my love, rubbing my hands up her bare legs.

"I told you I would make you pay for the car." Her teasing smile quickly melted away. "I'm sorry you have trouble with the Russians now."

I outlined Fiona's bottom lip with my thumb. "That wasn't your fault. Ivan would have found a way to force his hand sooner or later. What did you show his brother anyway?"

She smirked. "A picture of him with someone that was most definitely *not* his wife. The way the other two tried not to laugh, I'm sure some already know about his affair."

"Many mafia leaders have mistresses, what's the problem with that?"

"Yes, many of them do. But how many of them have a mister instead of a mistress?"

"Ah. Yes. I can see that being a problem. As the new pakhan, he is responsible for producing an heir. Can't happen without a woman."

Fiona leaned forward and kissed my chin. "A lot can't happen without a woman."

I chuckled and kissed her. "Why didn't you go back to sleep?"

She shrugged. "I sleep better with you there. I was just checking to see where you were when I saw you online looking for me." She was teasing me again, but I didn't care.

"Yes, I was curious because I hadn't ever seen your name on the approved list."

"Because it's not there."

I poked her in the stomach and made her squirm. "No, because you never gave me control back of my own company, like you said you did."

"I never said that. I told you I would let you back in, and I did." She bit her lip and moved away again. She twisted her hands nervously. "Are you mad?"

"No, not at all. I trust you. I know you have my back." I cursed when I saw a tear fall on her cheek. I brought her back to me and kissed it. "Why are you crying? What's wrong?"

"Nothing's wrong. I'm just more emotional lately. And no, before you ask, I am not pregnant. The IUD is still firmly in place."

I chuckled. "I know, princess." I placed my hand on her bare stomach and rubbed it softly. "But one day, I will convince you to let me put a baby in here. Until then, I am going to enjoy every minute I get with you, without the interruption of a child."

We were silent for a minute before Fiona spoke again, changing the subject. "So, this is the office, huh? Kind of bare."

I chuckled. "Like yours is much better? We don't do much here. It's mostly for private meetings or going through the money from our various activities."

"What about that window? Is it so you can keep an eye on everyone, or watch your half naked dancers in their cages?"

"They have cages?" I dramatically pretended to be ignorant of that. "I never noticed before. Keith must have put them in while I've been away."

She pushed against my chest and got up. "You're such a liar."

I watched as she walked over to the window and looked down. I followed soon after, never having been very good at keeping distance between us.

I stepped up behind Fiona, making sure she could feel every growing inch of me. "Look down at our kingdom, princess. This is my world. They party by my laws. I alone control their freedoms here. I choose who lives and dies. I choose who gains and who loses. They fear me, they respect me. Because I am their King."

As I spoke softly, I lightly dragged my fingers up and down her arm, then over her shoulder, and started making my way down her front.

"It is by my choice if they find the personal release they find here tonight. No matter the form it comes in. What about you, princess? What kind of release do you need? You are the only one this king will bow down to. You are the only one I will ever serve, I will ever worship. Let me worship you." I slowly pulled her sports bra off, her hair coming up with it. I then lowered myself to the floor, pulling the boy shorts down with me.

Fiona's hand fell on the glass for balance, as I kissed my way back up, stopping around the middle for a minute or two. Once I was up, I went behind her again, pushing her lower back enough so she would bend over.

"Look out over my kingdom, my love. Look at them, peasants compared to us. Look at them and know that we control what they do."

She screamed out a moan as I possessed her body.

"You control their cyber life. I control their physical one. Between the two of us, we can control it all. Together, we are all-knowing, we are all-powerful." My words helped push her over that edge at least once before I stopped talking.

After I got my release, I stepped back, nearly falling to the floor. Fiona huffed out a laugh as she turned around. She fell against the window, then curled a finger. Obeying her command, I joined her and kissed her.

"I love you."

I smiled and returned the sentiment against her lips. It wasn't long before I was lifting her leg and taking her again.

"How many people just saw us?" She asked after I finally lowered her back to the floor.

"Took you long enough to ask that. Zero. It's a one-way mirror."

"Have you…" Fiona blushed and turned away. I lifted her chin for another kiss.

"No. Only you. Only you have earned the privilege."

She sighed, relieved. "So, no one saw every part of me against this window?"

I laughed and shook my head.

"Well, one did. But I really don't think I count anymore."

I looked at the ceiling praying for patience. Fiona was not smiling when I looked down again. I tried to shrug and play it off.

"He has his kinks. I'm working on breaking them. It's a process."

She bent down and picked up her clothes before standing up and putting a finger in my face, and then pulling it back when I tried to bite it.

"Deal with him, or I will deal with you. Maybe I should just cut you off until you are done weaning him."

"Please don't do that. Anything but that." I begged like an idiot, ready to drop to my knees if I had to.

She left without saying a word. I just stood there staring at her like a moron. Of course, she was still naked, so it was a bit distracting.

Once the elevator had taken her away, I put my own pants on and sank onto a chair. "You are going to cost me dearly if you keep this up."

"Nah, she's getting over it. She didn't even bother trying to dress first this time."

I lifted my foot and kicked him. "Why should she? You literally just admitted to seeing all of her naked! What difference would it have made now?"

"See, a few more times and she won't care anymore."

"Keith… please?"

He chuckled. "I wasn't in here. I walked in right as she was asking. I wasn't even looking when she left. I just wanted to mess with you both."

I cursed. "You are going to be the death of me." I rubbed my face, part of me wanting to slug him. "Are they gone?"

"Nope, I talked them into staying for a private dance. On the house. It took some convincing, but they are in there now. Of course, if this window were see-through, everyone would have gotten a show."

I flipped him off and ran after my girl, praying she would believe me.

Chapter 19

Fiona

Nearly three weeks had passed since the Ivan incident. My face was mostly back to normal, just still a little tender at times, as was Dillan. He was still handsy, but not nearly as much. We were getting better at the cuddling without the molesting each other bit. We also were doing better at waiting for a private room.

We stayed at the studio for a couple days, that way he could catch up on some much-needed work, and not have to go far from me. After the visit from the Russians, he went into Uber-overprotective mode. He even doubled the guard on Randy. I also learned he had one on my Dad. I couldn't help but wonder how that went over.

I made a habit of joining him in the office at night. He even showed me where a speaker was if I wanted to listen to the music. We danced together every night - which always led to me against the window without my clothes. Dillan liked to tease Keith about his kinks, but he had them too.

Now, here I stood, staring at the elevator that would take me up to my office. I was excited to finally be back to work. Yet, I couldn't make myself push the dang button.

"Hey, you're back."

I did a jump spin, startled, and saw Chris walking up. "Oh, yeah. At least, I hope so. I have a meeting with the Senior Partners in a few minutes. You know… once I actually get up the guts to go up there. Do you think they are going to fire me?"

Chris laughed and called the elevator. Butthead. "No one has said anything one way or the other. Your office is still yours. Your secretary is still your secretary. There have been no signs of replacing you. Which they would have done by now if they were going to."

"That's true enough, I guess." I let him half drag me onto the elevator car, by the upper arm. "Unless they were waiting to officially talk to me."

He let go of me and pushed for our floor. "Yeah, but I doubt it. You're a valuable member of the team, Fi. We need you."

"Thank you. And thanks for helping Dillan when… you know."

He nodded and cleared his throat. "When did you, uh, start dating him?"

I hid the grimace. I wished I hadn't put off going upstairs. I could have avoided this conversation altogether. Or at least postponed it.

"Around the time I got promoted. We didn't start anything official until a couple of weeks later."

He nodded twice before speaking again. "Why did you lock him out of his own company?"

I laughed. He seemed incredulous about that, but at least he wasn't dwelling on the fact that I sort of dated them both for a week.

"It's a long story. Basically, it was because the night we met, he ticked me off by lying to me and being a sneak. So, I locked him out of everything digital. Just like most of the world, that means pretty much everything. His techie couldn't crack it, nor could they find me. They resorted to following my brother, who I meet every week for family dinner with our father. By the time I came out of the building, Dillan was there, fuming." I laughed. It was a good time.

"Then how…" He scratched his head, still confused.

I shrugged. "Who knows with men, you all don't make sense to us womenfolk." I teased and stepped off the elevator. The distraction had helped, and I was more relaxed now.

When I reached my office, Linda nearly knocked me over with her hug. We had messaged a few times but had not seen each other yet. She patted me down like a mother hen, inspecting me.

"I'm fine, Linda. Really."

She ended on my face, both hands holding my head as she took in every detail. "You look good, but that could be make-up."

I licked my finger and wiped it across my cheek. "You know I don't wear much."

She finally relaxed and let me go. "Alright. I won't badger you anymore. At least not right now. The Senior Partners are waiting in conference room B for you."

I cringed and looked down the hall, but the door was closed. "Any ideas which way the wind blows?"

"Not a clue, but you are a brave girl. You'll be fine." She spun me and pushed me to get me walking.

I huffed in annoyance at her. She didn't realize this was worse for me than dealing with Ivan.

I knocked on the conference room door and waited until Lawerence opened it. He was usually my direct line supervisor. His smile was there, but not as light as normal. My heart sank. They waved for me to take the seat at the end, all the way across from them.

I smiled, barely. Then I decided to hell with it. If they already had their minds made up, how did my behavior matter?

"So, what's the verdict? Am I being kicked to the curb because of my idiotic brother or because I fell for a moron who happens to own a club?"

Gary guffawed. "What?"

"My contract said that I could not associate with criminals while working here. My brother has a gambling problem, which he is finally seeking help for, and my boyfriend runs a club that the mafia frequents. He's not part of all that but likes to have a roof over his head. I'm not saying he is innocent - we all know that would be a lie after what happened a few weeks ago, but still. I broke my contract."

"I love this girl." Gary said in a sigh. "No, you are not being fired. As for the contract, that is more for those who would take advantage of their position here. We all know you don't do that."

"Eh. I kind of do." Oh, will you shut up, Fiona! Apparently once I got started… "I mean, mostly because hacking is fun, and you all seem to get a kick out of me freaking out the clients. Here I get to do it without getting in trouble. Although now I hack my boyfriend and his friends just for kicks and giggles. His IT guy thinks it's the best game ever." I cringed. "Sorry, I get mouthy and ramble when I'm nervous."

"I'd be curious to know what all you said to Ivan." Gary was still leading the charge.

I gulped. "It wasn't pretty. It nearly got me, and my brother killed. Or rather him killed and me a fate worse than death. I got a couple good shiners out of it though. Sorry, I'll shut up now."

"We asked for this meeting so we could talk about what happened." Kurt cut in, before Gary could get his next words out. He looked a little glum about that. "You were taken from our offices, right under our noses. We thought our background checks were good enough. It's not often that our own security system fails us."

Oh, cool. I could work with that.

I told them the story of going to pay off Dillan and locking him out (not the why, of course, that would be a bit too much info). I told them about Bunny and Ivan, and then how Ivan used my brother. I told them what Ivan wanted me to do, and how I got around him (I left out the tidy little nest egg I made for myself. I still found it funny that the Russians hadn't asked any questions about their missing money). Finally, I told them how we got out.

When I was done, they all looked at each other like they were having a silent conversation.

"We need to create a list of the major criminals in the area, at least." Lawerence said. "We can't promise safety for our employees if we aren't actually being safe."

I raised a finger part way into the air. "I can help with that. I actually have access to a database that tracks them all. Dillan can be a bit on the paranoid side, especially now. And I only gave him access again to his system, I never gave him control back. It's all good, he knows and doesn't seem to care. Not like he knows what to do with all that anyway." I cleared my throat like an idiot, trying to remember my point. "I, uh, can transfer that info over to the company server, which I promise only has me in the correct category for access permission. I've never messed with it here. Well, not completely anyway. I did do a little peeking around when I got hired. A girl has to be safe; ya know? I should probably shut up now."

Gary was doing a horrible job at hiding his amusement. The other two just looked at me like I had two heads.

I grimaced. "I'm fired now, aren't I?"

"No. As I said before, we're better off with you on our side." Lawerence looked like he wanted to laugh but wasn't sure if it was that kind of funny or not.

"How is your brother, Ms. Reynolds? Is he better now? And I remember your father had a heart attack recently, yes?" Kurt was always the killjoy.

"My Dad doesn't know much yet. We've been careful about what we tell him. I was sick and Randy had to work. Randy's surgery on his leg went well. He was released from the hospital a few days ago. We had a home health aide reserved for him before then. He will go visit our Dad when he doesn't look like he died and came back from hell. In the meantime, he seems to have finally had his wake-up call and has already started sessions with a therapist for his addiction. As for my Dad, he loves the nursing home. He's made many great friends. Thank you for asking."

"Good. Let us know if you need anything. And, please, if you wouldn't mind, send us that information."

I gave him a stupid thumbs up and high tailed it out of there. Linda and Chris were both waiting for me near my office.

"Don't you all have work to do? I know I do." I winked and stepped into my office.

Home sweet home.

Epilogue

Dillan

I exhaled before taking a swig of beer and picked the report up again. It was from the security team I had rotating around Randy. He didn't know it, but his home health aide was a former Army Corporal, dishonorably discharged. A fellow soldier had tried to take advantage of her while she was sleeping. If only he had known that she slept with a knife under her pillow.

She had great aim, even half-asleep.

Unfortunately for her, his father was a General. He didn't believe her claim and insisted she get some type of punishment. Her commanding officer believed her, but his hands were tied. He was at least able to keep the sentence down to a dishonorable discharge.

Randy was in good hands. Literally. She was strong enough to lift him if he fell, and tough enough to go drill sergeant on him when needed.

That wasn't what bothered me though. There was an increase in tourist traffic around his apartment building. Of the Russian kind.

Viktor had found him.

If I was being honest with myself, I always knew this day would come. I'd been wracking my brain for months trying to come up with a solution. Outside of selling my soul to the Italians, I couldn't think of anything else. I didn't have the might to go against the Bratva. Not yet. In a few years… maybe.

Keith and I were currently searching for a location for our next club, *Exposure*. I would need more personnel and more security. I would be doubling my own army. I wanted to better protect the family I was planning to create with Fiona.

She was at the hospital with Katia now, holding one of her hands while she birthed twin boys.

We were set to get married within the next month. I popped the question one week after we moved into our new house together. It sits on the beach. A private one. Where I proposed to her. She surprised me by saying she had her IUD removed the day before. The game was on now.

I just had to figure out how to better protect our family.

No matter how much I didn't want to, it looked like the Italians were going to be my only option. But I knew what Bruno would want. 65% of *my* company.

I lifted my head at the ding of the elevator, confused at who that could be. Fi was still at the hospital. BoBo had driven her there and was waiting for her. Jorge and Kent were on vacation together. And Keith should still be monitoring the fights. I was supposed to be too but couldn't focus so I came back here.

I slowly opened the top right drawer in my desk, reaching for my gun.

"I wouldn't do that if I were you." A deep voice called from the hallway. "We are just here to talk. We will come in when you remove your hand from that drawer. I'm not worried about our safety. I'm worried about yours. Fiona has suffered enough in her life. I wouldn't want her to lose you as well."

I dropped my gun and closed the drawer. "Who the hell are you?"

Two tall men entered my office, before I could even tell them I had put the gun away. When I looked at them curiously, the younger one tilted his phone back and forth, then pointed at the camera in the corner.

I gave them both an incredulous eyebrow as the older one sat down. The younger one stayed standing behind him. While he looked relaxed, I could tell he was far from it.

"How did you hack into my cameras? That should be impossible."

The younger man smirked. The older man snorted. "Nothing is impossible when it comes to my nephew. I will say this though. Your fiancé is probably the first to challenge him like she did. I thank you for that. Punk needed deflating."

The smirk on the nephew turned to a scowl.

"Guess that explains how you got access to my elevator too. Who are you?"

The older man placed his right ankle over his left knee, feigning comfort, and ease. Just like his nephew, it was an act.

"My name is Mitch Anderson. I am the underboss to the American Mafia on the West Coast."

My eyes widened. "Cooper?" I mentally cursed.

What the hell was going on now? How did I offend them? I'd never dealt with them before. They were headquartered in San Francisco, but I knew they had a presence here as well. They weren't as flamboyant about their dealings as the Russians and

Italians were. Even still, everyone knew they were there, hiding in the dark.

Mitch tipped his head in a silent nod. "Yes, the Coopers. And no, you did nothing wrong. You have not offended us in any way.

My heart stopped. How did he know what I was thinking?

This time it was Mitch that smirked. "We are incredibly good at reading people. I heard you and your people are as well."

I opened and closed my mouth, completely stunned by what was happening.

"Your club has always been of interest. But our men knew you were not interested in a partnership. So, out of respect, we have kept our distance. Still, we had our eye on you and yours, waiting for a foot in the door. Smirnov seems to have given us that. You are in a tough spot. You want to protect your family, but you don't know what the safest route is. A plight we all can understand."

I swallowed and leaned back, letting my body relax, since it was obvious they were not here to cause problems.

"How would you be able to help? What kind of deal are we looking at?"

"We want a partnership. We want to build our presence here in LA."

"You have a presence here in LA. And I don't want to lose control of my company. That would lead to more problems in the future. Ones I would have no control over. It's bad enough that the Russians and Italians already know my weak spots."

Mitch lifted a single eyebrow. "You call Fiona Reynolds a weak spot?"

I snorted. "No, not even close. But my enemies would be able to come to me through her. If not directly through her, then her father or her brother. Online, she is a powerhouse. Outside…"

Mitch nodded. "I understand. Which is one of the reasons Levi thought you might be ready to hear our offer now. We believe in family. We believe in protecting our family. We do not want them becoming a target because of what we do. We can help you with that."

I huffed and shook my head. "And cost me, what? What will I get from it? More enemies?"

Mitch dropped his foot to the floor and leaned over. "How much is the safety of your family worth? Is any price too steep to keep Fiona and the children you want with her safe?"

Well, when he put it like that… I closed my eyes for a brief moment. "There is nothing I wouldn't be willing to pay for that. What is your offer?"

Mitch leaned back in his chair again. "25% of your company."

My jaw dropped to the floor. That was not what I was expecting. "You only want 25%? Are you serious?"

"Yes. We don't need the money from your income. Besides, you do a successful job running both the club and your side hustles. We have no need to take over."

"Then what do you get out of this?"

"We get a stronger foothold here in LA. Even just that much will send a message to anyone who would come after your people. We will also help fill your ranks as you open the new club. If you wouldn't mind my opinion, the old warehouse near the garment district that you and Keith saw last night would be perfect."

I glanced up at the silent nephew, he stared back. If I wasn't used to the way Fiona randomly snooped around, I'd be unnerved. She had desensitized me to the way of hackers.

I nodded. "I could work with that. What else?" There had to be more that they wanted.

Mitch tipped his head up, indicating his nephew. "He and a few other boys will start at UCLA this Fall. We want them working, not partying. We taught them the skills, and we don't want them going to waste. It will also help us to know they are in a safe place, with people looking out for them. Not so much Noah here, but some of the others. I know my wife would appreciate him having someone looking out for him."

This time, the boy reacted. He rolled his eyes, but the touched smile was there.

"I can definitely work that. I was already planning on sending half my crew over to the new club when it opens. Then splitting the new blood between the two."

"Good, we can send a few more boys down that weren't planning on college this year."

"So many boys that are so young. Will they be able to handle all of this? Working in a club isn't for the faint of heart. They need to know what they are doing."

Mitch chuckled, moving to stand up as he opened a briefcase I hadn't noticed he had set on the floor.

"Don't worry, they are very well trained. You will not have any problems with them. If you do, have BoBo teach them a lesson. They are used to the consequences of failure."

Right.

Mitch handed me a contract all written up. I glimpsed inside the briefcase before he closed it.

"How many contracts are you all making while you are in town?"

"Just this one." He set the contract on my desk. "We were prepared with a variety of deals for you. I had planned to start higher, but after spending the last two days in your club and city, I decided we didn't need it. I thought this was the best deal."

"How had I not noticed you here before tonight?"

I vaguely saw Noah step away from his uncle while Mitch pointed out where I needed to sign, when I looked up again, the kid was gone. I searched the room with my eyes, then jumped when the kid stepped out next to me.

"We know how to blend into the shadows, Mr. Murphy." Noah said quietly. "That's why you didn't see us."

Okay. Good call. Glad I chose these guys over the Italians.

Mitch put his hand in front of me. "Welcome to the Cooper family, Dillan. And don't worry about the Russians anymore. They've been taken care of, and a message has been sent."

"What? How?"

With knowing smiles, both men left my office, only to be intercepted by a glowing Fiona coming out of the elevator. They nodded and smiled politely as they passed her. She smiled back, confused. Then she saw me and began telling me in detail about the beautiful little girls that just came into the world. Apparently, the doctors had misread the sonogram pictures. Katia whined. Andy was perfectly happy.

Fiona was just taking a breath and asking about my visitors when a message came in on my phone.

Babysitter: Thought you'd like to know. The Russians' car just blew sky high. One block away. Two new men are stationed outside. They said the family sent them. They look like teenagers. What the hell did you do?

Fiona was already searching up the camera footage from outside her brother's building. We both watched as a man, no more than a kid really, practically slid under the car before popping back out. No one blinked an eye. 5 minutes later. Boom.

Me: I made a deal. To protect us all. It was the best of the lot.
Babysitter: With who?
Me: The Cooper Family.

I watched as the conversation dots appeared and disappeared repeatedly.

Babysitter: What have I gotten myself into? I hope you know what you are doing.

So, did I.

***

To the outside world, Edgemont High is your typical high school. Well, not exactly typical. They once had the worst reputation in the country. Before Levi Cooper came along, it was run by the local gangs.

A few years later, that is no longer the case. Unbeknownst to the public, it is now run by the American Mafia.

These men have many rules they live by. Loyalty and trust are at the top. But their highest and most important rule, no one messes with their family. Especially their women. They'd burn their way through hell to protect what belongs to them.

Wanna know more about those Coopers? Check out *The Cooper Family Chronicles* by TJ Lee

ABOUT THE AUTHOR

TJ is an avid reader. Reading was always an escape for her in her crazy messed up world. She's always had a vivid imagination. It wasn't until she was locked in her house for a year and a half, with only her two young kids, and two dogs to talk to, that she finally started writing. She found an even better escape.

TJ is a High School English teacher and a single mom. She holds a Bachelor's degree in Cultural Anthropology and Master's in Cultural Responsive Education. Her life motto, one she says with her students regularly, is to "fly your weird flag high!" She wants everyone to learn to be true to who they are. Accept yourself the way you are. Love yourself the way you are.

9 789898 999838